With You

THE COMPLETE SERIES

JESSICA MADDEN

ISBN: 978-0-646-88909-2

For Leonie

ONE WHOLE NIGHT WITH YOU

Chapter One

Justin walks into the café half an hour before my shift ends. I press his order on the register before he even reaches the counter.

He takes out his wallet with a knowing, familiar smile. "Would you like anything else with the latte?" I ask, pointing to the display of muffins, cupcakes, iced donuts, and banana bread in the cabinet beside me.

Justin glances at the displays. "Blueberry muffin, thanks Amberlee."

He taps the eftpos machine with his card after I send it through. I let my co-worker, Stacey, make his coffee while I plate Justin's muffin and follow him to his favourite table near the front counter. Taking in his unusually formal shirt and tie, I remember that he had a job interview this morning.

"How did it go?" I ask, tilting my head.

Justin nods, prioritising ripping off the paper on his muffin and takes a huge bite of it over speaking. Knowing Justin like I do, it's a good sign.

"It went well," he says while chewing. He swallows it before continuing to speak. "I find out on Monday if I get it."

I smile at him. Justin has been struggling to look for a job for a year, but has never had any luck. Hopefully, this time he will be able to score himself a paid gig while he studies. "That's great, Justin. I'm pretty sure you will get it. Who wouldn't want to you around five days a week?"

He laughs, his blue eyes lighting up. "I hope so too."

Stacey calls out his order, and I retrieve it for him before returning to work behind the counter.

I serve a few more people before my shift is over. Justin waits for me outside while I help my co-workers clean up and closed.

"So, what are your plans with Oliver tomorrow?" Justin asks me as we walk down the street together towards the tram stop. "Doing anything special for your first Valentine's Day?"

I smile at the mention of my boyfriend's name, despite the slightly off tone of his voice. "I have no idea what we are doing. He hasn't told me what the plans are. He is probably going to surprise me with something."

"I'm sure he will."

"What about you? Have you found someone to take out?"

Justin shakes his head as we cross the road to the tram station. "Nope. Even if I did, you know I don't really care much for the whole "valentine" thing. I just don't understand why you need to show the person you love how much you mean to them on that day. And why you need to spend twice as much on a dozen roses than you would on any other day of the year."

"Yeah, yeah," I say, a wrinkle forming in my nose. It isn't the first time we've had this conversation. "What are you planning to do for the night then?"

Justin's face lights up. "You know what I'm doing. I'm seeing Night Rangers play at the Melbourne Arena tomorrow."

I had completely forgotten Justin's favourite band was playing tomorrow night, my favourite band, too, if I'm being honest. I wanted to go with him, but with it being Valentine's Day, I wanted to spend it with my boyfriend; our first Valentine's Day together. Five months into our relationship, and even though it seemed like we were rushing, it just felt right with Oliver.

The tram stops in front of us. The doors open and a couple of people get off. We step on and hold onto the rails of the already packed tram.

"I wish I could go with you," I say.

"You still can. Just tell Oliver you can't make it. He hasn't even made sure you're free… and it's Night Rangers, Amberlee. Night Rangers."

"I can't tell him that! It's our first Valentine's Day."

"Valentine's Day is overrated. I mean, why do you need February fourteenth to show the person you love how much they mean to you? Even if you don't go on a date tomorrow, you have the other three hundred and sixty four days to go on one and be celebrated."

The tram doors close and the driver rings the bell before moving the tram along.

"I feel that it's supposed to be a special day," I say. "It's romantic and intentional. Besides, if you treated a girl like it was Valentine's Day on a normal Saturday, I bet she'd think you were about to propose!"

"Every day is a special day with the person you love," he replies with a shrug, looking at his shoes.

I nod, knowing he was right, and that I'd never win this argument with him. "True."

Even though Justin seemed like he wasn't a romantic person who couldn't give a stuff, he really was sweet when it came to showing someone how much he cared about them. Two ended with him getting dumped on Valentine's Day, so I sometimes wondered if part of the reason he hated the day was because of that. He hasn't dated anyone seriously since we graduated high school.

But I know, too, that Justin's never really been keen on Oliver. To keep the peace, he is polite, but

never initiates talking to him. He has never really told me the reason why he disliked him, but I appreciate him being kind. It's one of the things I love about Justin. He will always be kind to someone even when he doesn't like them. It's why I never really fully understood why no girl wanted to be with him. Especially because he really does have the best, sweetest personality in a not unattractive package.

"Are you only wanting me to come to the concert because you don't exactly want me to go on a date with Oliver?" I couldn't help but ask.

Justin doesn't answer me at first. The tram slows to a stop at the next station. The doors open and a few people get off before the next lot of people come on.

"I never said I didn't want you to go on a date with him," he answers once the tram begins moving again. "I'm happy for you, Amberlee, to be with someone you truly love. Yeah, I would love it if you could come along with me to see my favourite band perform, but I know how much this date means to you, too."

I smile, wondering what I would ever do without Justin. "Why don't we do something on Sunday night? It will just be you and me. We don't get to do much together since we graduated school. I work part-time on top of studying and since I moved in with Oliver, I really haven't been coming out as much. And all your spare time is spent on the job hunt so you can escape your parents' house. So what do you say? Should we hang out on Sunday? It can be our belated Best Friend's Valentine's Day date."

Justin smiles brightly. "Sounds great to me. Make me jealous of your plans tonight? I'm writing cover letters. Or an essay on marketing models."

I shrug. It wasn't something my boyfriend and I have actually talked about. Most nights we would cuddle up on the couch and watch Netflix for most of the night, staring at our respective laptops instead of talking.

"Nothing much I don't think," I say.

* * *

The front door is unlocked when I get home. The house is quiet. Usually, when I return home from work, Oliver is listening to his favourite rock bands, or he is cooking up a meal in the kitchen. Tonight he was not doing any of that. Perhaps he was taking a shower?

I call out to Oliver as I walk to the bathroom, but it's opened ajar and there is no one in there.

That's when I hear someone curse. Someone was in our bedroom.

"Oliver?" I call out again. "Is everything alright?"

I walk over to the bedroom. The door is fully opened and that's when I see the naked woman scrambling to grab her scattered clothes off the floor. Oliver, trying to look innocent, to pretend what I was seeing was not happening, was standing beside *our* bed with his jeans around his ankles.

"Amberlee, hi. This isn't what it looks like."

Chapter Two

"Who is she?" I ask Oliver. The woman is gone, chased out of our home by my sickening horror and Oliver's apologetic grimace.

He hesitates before answering, "She's nobody."

I shake my head. "No. Don't lie to me, Oliver. She *is* somebody."

He doesn't look at me as he says his next words. "Hilary is in my class. She came over so we could work on a project together."

A lump forms in my throat and I was doing all I could to fight back tears. How could this be happening right now? How could I have not seen that he was sneaking around my back with someone else? Oh, I can see why he cheated on me for that woman. Hilary is gorgeous – tall, slim, and blonde.

I wasn't blonde, but I knew Oliver had a thing for blonde women. Maybe I should have taken it as a sign when we first began dating. It shouldn't have mattered, really, with who he preferred to date. In the end we never really end up dating someone with the traits we would like them to be. I just keep trying to justify and make excuses for why he'd do this. I shake my head to clear the thought. There wasn't an excuse.

"Bull crap, Oliver."

This time he glances at me, the guilt showing in his dark eyes. But it was all too late for that now. He has ruined our relationship.

We are done. Finished. Finito. Over.

He can start apologising and begging me to take him back, but I'm not going to be a fool and do it. I'm better than that. Right?

"I'm sorry, Amberlee." He takes a step towards me, but I step back. "I swear nothing is going on with me and Hilary."

I feel the blood rising in me and my eyes pricked with tears.

"Nothing is going on between you two?!" I almost scream. "Remind me again, why you were having sex on our bed when I walked in if nothing going on between you two?"

He opens his mouth, then closes it. Opens and closes. And I can't hold the tears back anymore.

I let them fall. I am so damn stupid for not seeing that he was cheating on me.

Only, there was no way of telling that he was. I mean, he never stayed back late at uni, and he always came straight home after his shift at McDonald's. I've never seen him engrossed on his phone, or leaving the room to text or call someone. He always paid attention to me.

So why didn't I see he was with someone else?

Oliver steps forward again, ready to wrap me into a hug, like I was going to accept it after what he had just done to me.

I aggressively shove him hard in the chest. "Get away from me!"

"I just want to say I'm sorry, Amberlee. I should never have asked Hilary over here."

I shake my head. "Don't say you're sorry because you are not. If you were sorry, you wouldn't have gone behind my back to be with some other woman. How long have you been screwing *that* whore? You're so damn pathetic, you know that, Oliver? What? You didn't have the balls to break up with me?"

"She's my ex-girlfriend. We got back together last month. I'm sorry, Amberlee. I should have told you. I wasn't even supposed to get back with her. It just happened."

My heart crumbles to pieces hearing this.

"A month?" I grind my teeth together. "A whole freaking month?!"

Before I can think about my actions, I raise my hand and smack Oliver across his face. My palm burns from the impact of his skin and a red mark is left on his cheek.

I point to the bedroom door. "Get. Out. Of. This. House."

"Amberlee."

"I said get out!" I scream at him this time. "Get your things and get out! I want all of your belongings gone by tomorrow!"

Oliver doesn't move. "I don't have anywhere to go."

"Well, maybe you should have freaking thought about it before you cheated on me, you jerk!"

I shove him hard in the chest again.

"Okay!" He holds his hands up in surrender. "I will call up some mates to see if they can take me in for the night. I will be back tomorrow to get the rest of my things."

He goes to the wardrobe and pulls out a duffel bag.

I leave the room and curl up on the couch, letting the tears fall. I was sure all of this was some kind of nightmare, but that wasn't what the ache in my chest tells me. Over my sobs I can hear Oliver opening and closing drawers as he stuffs his clothing into his bag. It takes him ten minutes to gather some clothes and then he comes out to the lounge room. Before he walks out the front door, he reminds me that he will be back tomorrow to get the rest of his belongings, like I hadn't heard him say it the first time.

Frankly, I don't even want to be here when he comes back. Luckily, I have a shift in the morning so I don't have to see his face.

I should have taken Justin's advice when he told me I shouldn't move in with Oliver after dating him for three months. I was sure Oliver and I were going to take a huge step for the future when we decided this.

I feel like a fool. I can almost hear Justin telling me I'm not, knocking his shoulder with mine. I know. I know he won't say 'I told you so', he'll just be here with me. I don't want anything else right now, just his company.

I pull out my phone and message him.

Can you come over? Oliver and I have just broken up. I add a sad face emoji with a single tear down one side of its face.

Justin replies within seconds. **Are you serious?! What happened, Am?**

I wipe my eyes before I type my answer. **I will explain when you get here.**

* * *

Justin gets here within an hour. He comes with two 500mL tubs of gourmet chocolate ice cream. I have only been through one break up (now two), and I remember when the first guy broke my heart, Justin went out of his way to get ice cream for the both of us. We sat together, ate the ice cream, and made each other laugh to make me feel better, forgetting about the idiot who had broken my heart. I never told him, though, that being with him was enough for me to feel better than a tub of chocolate ice cream ever could.

As soon as I let him into the house, he embraces me. He holds me for a long time before he tells me to sit down on the couch and goes into the kitchen for spoons. I do as he says and sit down. I hear him going through the kitchen drawers.

While I wait for him to return, I pull out my phone and go through the photo gallery on my phone. I just don't understand what went wrong in the relationship. Oliver and I were happy... at least, I thought we were.

"Put your phone away, Amberlee," Justin says as he comes to sit down beside me, holding the two tubs with the head of the spoon dig into the ice cream to hold it up. "There is no use looking back at the photos and making yourself sadder."

He was right, but I couldn't help it. I listen to him sighing as I put my phone on the coffee table, and then take the tub Justin holds out to me. I thank him and place a spoonful of ice cream into my mouth.

"So, do you want to tell me what happened with this jerk?" he asks when I don't offer the information.

I lick some ice cream off my spoon before I answer him, recalling the moment I saw the woman in our room. It brought the tears back, and I couldn't get the words I wanted to say out. Justin puts an arm around me and leans me into him. I sob loudly onto his shoulder. He rubs his hand up and down my arm, soothing me.

When the sobs started to subside, I wipe my eyes and sit up straight. "He cheated on me… with his ex-girlfriend."

Justin shakes his head. "What a jerk."

"I know! I don't even know what I did wrong to make him feel the need to cheat on me. Why did he picked his ex over me?" I stab my spoon into the ice cream and just let it sit there. "I can't believe I never saw this coming."

There's silence between us for a few minutes until Justin makes me face him.

"Don't blame yourself for anything, Am. It's not your fault. It's Oliver's. He is the one who decided to go behind your back with another woman. If he still had feelings for his ex, then he should have been upfront with you."

"I should have known he was cheating on me, but he showed no signs that he was. Aren't there supposed to be signs? But there was nothing."

"He is a jerk. No, more like a douchebag. What kind of idiot chooses someone who'd knowingly have an affair with someone over gorgeous, kind you? Honestly, right now I want to go and punch his face in, but I won't because I don't want to be charged with assault."

I smile at him, my cheeks stiffer than usual with the salt from my tears. "You know you don't have to ever do that for me. If anyone is punching him in the face, it should be me. I should have listened to you in the first place when you told me not to move in with him. It was too soon and I should have waited longer."

He puts his arm around me and pull me closer to him so my head is resting on his shoulder again.

"I would do anything for you, Amberlee. You're my best friend. I don't want to ever see you get hurt. And don't be so hard on yourself. You did what you thought was right. Oliver is the one who chose to make the wrong decision."

I pull back so I can give him a small smile. "You're right, Justin. And thank you for being my friend. I don't know what I would do without you."

He gently rubs my arm. "Why don't we sit back and watch a good chick flick on Netflix, eat our ice cream before it melts, and forget about Oliver? It may not fully take away the heartache, but forgetting just for a little while will help."

I agree to his suggestion. I may never have had a girl-friend to sit back and watch chick flicks with, or other things you may do when you break up with someone, but I was glad that Justin was able to put up with all of this girly stuff. Even if it was for just one night.

And one night is all I really needed from him to feel better.

Chapter Three

I had no energy to get out of bed the next morning. Just knowing it was Valentine's Day made me want to stay in bed all day and cry. Pathetic, I know. Only I couldn't because I had work this morning. But the thought of going into work at a café, I was bound to get caught up in a conversation with customers about what their romantic plans for the day, or seeing couples come into the café, cuddling, kissing and holding hands. I couldn't bear to see that without even thinking about Oliver.

I call my boss, telling him I'm not feeling well today. Then, I went back to sleep.

My vibrating phone stirs me awake. I pick it up to see who was calling me. I thought it would be Justin checking up on me to see how I was, but no. It was Oliver. What does this jerk want?

I answer and my heart sinks in my chest when I hear his voice.

"I was wondering if I could come over this morning to grab my stuff," he says. "My mates are coming over to help me."

I wished I had gone to work this morning. I wouldn't have to see his face then. But I knew I had to let him come over to get the rest of his belongings. I did say I wanted him out by today, after all.

Once I got off the phone, I force myself to get out of bed. I search for a clean set of clothes and freshen myself up in the shower. Oliver arrives shortly after I had gotten out and I let him inside. It was odd to open the door to his knock. Two of his friends were with him, following him into the bedroom with cardboard boxes to pack his belongings.

I made myself a cup of tea. I hear Oliver and his friends talking, asking what belonged to him and what didn't. One even asked him how could he be so stupid to bring his ex (or now girlfriend, I supposed) over here. Oliver just replied that he didn't think. It made me wonder how many times he has brought her over here.

I was thankful that my phone rang then, distracting me for a moment. I smile when I see Justin's name flash across the screen.

"Hey, Justin," I greet him, placing my cup of tea down on the kitchen counter.

"Good morning. I'm just calling to see how you are from last night. I was hoping to catch up with you at work, but it turns out you aren't there."

Damn. I forgot Justin often comes into the café in the morning before he goes off to hand out his resume to businesses.

"I didn't feel up to going in today, so I called in sick," I tell him. "Besides, being there will get me down when all everyone will talk about is Valentine's Day."

"True, true."

"I also have Oliver over here."

There is a pregnant pause.

"What is that douchebag doing there? He hasn't hurt you enough?"

"He has his friends with him to gather up his belongings. They shouldn't be here for too long."

"Would you like me to come over? I have nothing to do today. Mostly all I'm doing is preparing for the concert."

I nod, smiling. "I would like that."

I hang up the phone just as Oliver and his friends walk by the kitchen, carrying a box each with my ex-boyfriend's belongings. They headed out the front door without even acknowledging me. I cross to the lounge room, peeking out the window to see the boys placing the boxes into the small hatchback, so I guess only two boxes could fit because they ended up closing the boot, and placed the third box into the backseat. They headed back inside to get the rest of Oliver's stuff.

I went back to the kitchen so they wouldn't think I was spying on them. I finished my tea while they disappear out of my sight again. It wasn't long before Justin shows up, already wearing his Night Rangers t-shirt.

He hugs me in greeting once I let him inside. "Hey, how are you doing?"

I nod. "I am okay."

He pulls away to inspect me. "You know you don't have to lie to me. It's okay to say you aren't okay. You have just gone through a break up, Am."

I give him a small smile. "I'm trying not to think about it. I promise you that I am feeling okay. A little hollow, I guess, but okay. And now you're here."

I shrug as he returns the smile and rubs a hand up and down my arm.

"That's good to hear."

Justin drops his hand as soon as Oliver and his friends walk into the lounge room again, each of them carrying a box. Oliver's friends walk out the door without even saying one word to me. Oliver, though, stops in front of me.

"Well, that's the last of my things," he tells me.

I nod. "Good."

He looks over at Justin. "Hey, Justin. How are you doing?"

Justin gives him a nod. "I'm good. So, I heard you got back with your ex."

Oliver looks over at me for a second, like he couldn't believe that I went and told my best friend what had happened. Of course I told him. I tell Justin everything.

Oliver turns back to Justin. "Yeah, I did. We weren't even planning to get back together. It just happened."

"And I guess you just forgot to mention it to Amberlee, hey? Busy schedule like yours," Justin says, his tone polite, his lip almost curling in a sneer. I can read every microexpression on Justin's face after fifteen years of friendship, but Oliver can't, and he doesn't know how to respond.

The three of us stand there in silence. All I wanted was for Oliver to leave, but he was still standing around like I never caught him cheating on me.

"Listen, Amberlee, I'm really sorry you had to find out about Hilary and I this way," he tells me. "I… I was going to tell you about us. I just didn't know how to. I hope you can forgive me."

He wanted me to forgive him for never telling me sooner about him getting back with his ex? How was I supposed to forgive him for not being honest with me; for cheating on me for a whole month? It's something I didn't know how to do. Forgiving him will probably take some time. He had stabbed my heart, and forgiving him was not in my best interest right now. And honestly, he didn't deserve it.

I shake my head as tears prickled my eyes. "Just go, Oliver. I don't want to ever see you again."

He nods. "Goodbye, Amberlee. Maybe I will see you around?"

Seeing you around is the last thing I want, I say silently to myself.

Without another word, Oliver leaves the house.

Once he is gone, I couldn't hold the tears in anymore. I break down in front of Justin, who embraces me, rubbing a hand up and down my back as I sob into his shoulder.

"It's okay, Am," Justin tells me. "He is out of your life now. He can't hurt you again."

I feel a pinch in my heart when he says this. "I was always hoping he will be in my life forever."

"What Oliver did to you was low. He doesn't deserve you, Amberlee."

I pull away from him, wiping my eyes. "I feel like such a fool. I was really hoping to have a great time today with him for our first Valentine's Day. Instead, I got dumped and humiliated."

"You know what, you should come along with me to see Night Rangers. It will be better than moping around here about

Oliver. Don't let him think he can ruin your day – Valentine's or otherwise."

I smile, nodding my head. "You're right, Justin. But are you sure you want me to come along to the concert? I mean, isn't it sold out?"

Justin nods. "It is. But lucky for me I bought two tickets."

"Two? Why? Were you planning to bring someone along?"

"The second ticket was for you," Justin admits, a little sheepish. "I was hoping you would come along to the concert. I knew you would most likely have a date with Oliver, but I got one just in case. So, what do you say? Would you like to go with me?"

There was no way I could turn down my best friend's offer. I have been wanting to see Night Rangers perform for so long, and this was my chance to see the band we'd loved more than air in high school live.

"I have an idea," Justin says once I agree. "When we go to the concert together, you must not ever mention Oliver. Got it?"

I nod, promising him I wouldn't. I chewed my lip, hoping I could keep that promise.

"Tonight is going to be us having a good time. There's no being miserable because you don't have a Valentine's date. We aren't even going to think about Valentine's Day. As far as I'm concern, it's a normal Saturday night. We will go to the concert, and make the most of the night. I want you to have the best night you have ever had," Justin says, soothing my worries away.

I nod, smiling. "Thanks, Justin. You're the best friend ever."

Chapter Four

Later that afternoon we head over to Justin's to get ready for the concert. He had a spare Night Rangers' shirt and lent it to me for the concert. Before we leave to head into Melbourne, Justin takes a photo of us wearing the shirts and posts it to social media.

We catch a tram into the city and head to Melbourne Arena, joining the long line up to get inside. The excitement builds up inside me, and I was happy Justin had brought me along rather than letting me mope around the house. If there is going to be anything to snap me out of my break up blues with Oliver, besides Justin, it will be Night Rangers. They have always been a band that cheered me up.

We grab snacks from the fast food outlets and find our seats in the second level, getting a great view of the stage.

While we wait for the supporting act to come on before Night Rangers, I couldn't help but take out my phone and stare at it. Even though I knew Oliver wasn't going to text me, half of me still hoped he would. Telling me that he has gotten it wrong about his ex, and that I'm the girl for him. But that was just wishful thinking. He was never going to message me and tell me he still wanted me. He was probably on a date with Hilary right this instant. And if he had been sneaking around with her, was he even going to ask me on a date tonight?

But then again, would I even want to take him back if he was to suddenly realise he had made a mistake?

No. I couldn't take him back. What if he was to do it again? I mean, once a cheater, always a cheater, right? I didn't want my heart to be broken for the second time.

"He isn't going to text you, Amberlee," Justin tells me. It doesn't surprise me that he read my mind. "He has made a decision that you aren't the girl he wants to be with. Which is a crappy, stupid decision, but then he's a douchebag and you deserve better."

I nod, sadly. "I know. I just... I just wish it didn't end the way it did."

Justin puts his hand over mine. "I know it hurts, Am. I wish it didn't end for you like this too. But remember our deal tonight?"

I nod. "You told me not to think about Oliver, and that tonight it's going to be about us having a great time."

He smiles at me. "Put the phone away for now. Don't check your phone for messages unless it's someone other than Oliver."

I agree to do so. It was hard to, but it was all for the best if I want to be able to enjoy tonight.

"I'm glad I have you here with me, Justin. Without you, I'm pretty sure I may not have been able to leave my bed."

He smiles and puts an arm around me. "That's what friends are for, Amberlee."

I return the smile.

"Hey, the opening act should be opening soon. Would you like a beer before it starts?" he asks.

I answer yes, and he gets up to go and get us a drink. He returns just as the lights dim, and a band I never heard of comes onto the stage. The backdrop behind the four band members reads 'Summer Heartbreakers'. Normally, I didn't like the opening acts, but this band really impressed me from the very first note. I bob to their music, enjoying every moment of it.

And what are the odds of a band with 'heartbreakers' in their name showing up to a gig on Valentine's Day? For a moment, I feel a slight stab in my heart, thinking about yesterday. But I quickly brush off the feeling, wanting this to be a night Justin and I can always remember. I wanted to remember it as a time when we had a great night out, and not when I was miserable because I had broken up with my boyfriend.

Besides, I was enjoying too much of the music to feel miserable over Oliver.

The band continued on for half an hour before they left the stage. I can't help but feel disappointed seeing them leave when I was really enjoying their music. Justin gives me permission to take my phone out to make a note of the band so I can look them up later. He watches over my shoulder like a helicopter parent, making me laugh as I do so and making sure I don't check my messages.

With time to spare until the Night Rangers come onto the stage, Justin gets up and buys us another round of drinks.

"You really don't need to be buying me any drinks," I tell Justin when he returns. "You already brought me the first one. I don't mind buying my own next time."

Justin takes a sip of his beer. "I know I don't need to. I want to buy you a drink, Am. I'm the one who is taking you out. Anything to make you feel good after that douchebag let you down."

He smiles, turning away from me to look out at the stage as the stage production crew were setting up for the Night Rangers. He takes another sip of his drink.

"I thought you said we weren't going to mention anything about him?" I ask, something

feeling different between us tonight.

He shrugs. "I didn't say his name. But forget I even mentioned it."

I smile, taking a sip of my beer. "You can resist all you want, Justin, but when the concert is over, I'm going to buy you a drink."

He turns to me. "Amberlee, really. There is no need for you to do that. I'm the one who is taking you out, remember?"

"And I want to be able to buy the next round of drinks to thank you for bringing me out here."

He considers this for a moment. "Alright. I will let you choose where we go after the concert."

"Deal."

It's not until another half an hour before the Night Rangers came onto the stage. Together, Justin and I sing at the top of our lungs along with the band.

Being here with Justin at this concert was better than any

Valentine's Day date. For a moment, this realisation gives me a pang of guilt. I dismiss it, because hanging out with Justin is always going to be one of my favourite things.

Chapter Five

I had a hint of sadness as the Night Rangers walked off the stage once the concert was over an hour and a half later. The concert was awesome and I didn't want it to end.

"This has been an awesome night, Justin," I say as we walk out of the arena together. "Thank you so much for convincing me to come out tonight."

"It's no problem, Amberlee. I just couldn't leave you at home alone after the break up. At least coming out to the concert gets you out of the house and doing something."

"What will I ever do without you?" I say, swinging my arm around his shoulders.

He smiles at me. "Definitely, I don't think you could survive without me. So, where to now? The night isn't over yet, and I doubt you even want to go home. You get to pick our next destination. I believe there was something about buying me a drink?"

My eyes did hurt from being tired, but I was afraid if I was to go home, how would I be without Justin there? I knew that once I get home I'm going to cry, maybe check my phone, hoping that maybe Oliver has changed his mind over everything. Being out here with Justin, I was enjoying his company and I didn't want the night to be over.

We get onto a tram and get off in the CBD. There was one place we have been to a few times that was still opened at this hour, and we headed down to the river. I order a pink gin spritz and Justin's completely unironic passion fruit margarita, and we sit down on the wooden tables. The restaurant was out in the open, and it was a perfectly clear night.

"You know, even though I didn't go on a date with Oliver tonight, this I have to say has been the best night of my life. It's better than any Valentine's Day date." I sip on my drink.

Justin smiles at me as he takes a sip of his own drink. "Do you remember in high school how we would spend Valentine's Day together?"

I nod, remembering the days of high school with him. He had always been my best friend since my family moved in next door to him when I was four. We were inseparable. When our high school would send around roses for Valentine's Day, Justin and I were always each other's Valentine's admirers. It never really bothered us. We didn't really start dating until after we turned sixteen. Justin started first before I entered the dating scene. None of us ever really been in a relationship longer enough to actually have a date for the fourteenth of February. Instead of going on dates, we would go to each other's houses and stay up late watching movies.

Just like what Justin is doing for me now with my break up with Oliver, when his girlfriends had chosen to break up with him on Valentine's Day, I always spent the night with him and cheered him up.

"I loved those nights," I say, smiling at the memories. "You know, as much as I was hoping to spend the night with Oliver, I'm really happy that I'm spending Valentine's with you."

"I'm glad to hear that."

We ordered another round of drinks before leaving the restaurant, walking along the riverside. It was after midnight. Valentine's Day was over, and I didn't want to head home any time soon. In fact I was enjoying my time with Justin so much that I didn't want this night to end at all.

"It's such a beautiful night," I say as we made our way towards the tram stop.

Justin nods. "I agree. Now, aren't you glad you came out with me? If you had stayed home moaning over Oliver, you wouldn't be out here on this wonderful night."

I laugh at his teasing expression and the genuine affection in his eyes. "You're right, Justin. I have you to thank for that. You have made this Valentine's Day one of the best, even if it didn't involve a date, a nice dinner, roses and chocolate."

Justin smiles, moving closer to me. "Pretty sure we only need each other to be happy, Amberlee. The roses and whatever are great, but when it's you and me, everyday is awesome, right?"

"You're right," I agree and loop my arm through his.

We walk beside the river in silence for a moment. It was so quiet out here with hardly any people around and less traffic now that it was after midnight. It was peaceful.

"So shall we head home now?" Justin asks me as we cross

the road to the tram station.

My body felt tired, but for some reason I just didn't feel like calling it a night right now. I wanted to stay out here with Justin as long as I could.

"Can we go to St. Kilda?" I suggest. "We could go down to the beach?"

Justin smiles as the tram that takes us to St. Kilda slowly pulls into the stop. "Sounds perfect for a midnight stroll on the beach."

We hop onto the tram and take a seat in the almost empty carriage.

I lean on Justin, resting my head on his shoulder as the tram moves along, heading down to the beach area. When we get there, we walk from the tram stop to the beach. We walk in silence down the empty street. Never have I thought I would be out here so late at night with my best friend.

"We should do this more often," I say.

"Do what?"

"Stay out late like this. We have never gotten to do this before."

"That's because we were in high school and we had curfews. Now that we are nineteen, we have no curfew. And yes, I would like to do this again sometime." He gives me a smile.

I return it as we reach the boardwalk. And as soon as I breathe in the salty sea air, I want to strip down and run into the ocean. Maybe it was the alcohol that was making me feel like this. I don't know. All I know is that I wanted to go for a swim, even if it was a bit cool.

"Come on, let's go for a swim," I say to Justin.

"You want to go for a swim at this time of the night?" he

says. "Are you crazy, Amberlee?"

I give him a cheeky smile. "Maybe."

I race across the sand with Justin behind me. When I was near the water, I take off the Night Rangers t-shirt and drop it on the sand. Justin stands beside me, watching me.

"What are you doing?" he asks me, his voice oddly strained.

"What does it look like I'm doing? I'm getting undressed."

I kick off my shoes and then unbuckle my jeans.

Justin looks around us. "You should put your clothes back on before someone sees you."

I laugh, pushing my jeans down and step out of them. "Relax, Justin. It's just us. The only person who is going to see me in my underwear tonight is you. That's if you are okay with that. I'm sure you don't want me to get your shirt wet." I know I'm taunting him with a dare, but it feels less playful than normal and I can't bring myself to stop.

He is trying his best not to look at me. "Okay. You win, Amberlee."

He takes off his shirt and drops it beside his feet. He strips down until he is only wearing his underwear and then I take off towards the water, screaming at the top of my lungs as soon as my feet splashes through the freezing cold water. Justin does the same when he enters.

He curses. "Why do you have to make me do this, Amberlee?"

I shrug, laughing. "I didn't make you do anything."

When we were knee deep, not wanting to go out further in case of sharks and riptides in the dark water, Justin splashes freezing cold water at me. I squeal, and then return the gesture. We do this a couple of times before he grabs my waist and spins me around. Over my squeals, I laugh. We stay in the water for a few minutes until our feet were beginning to go numb from the cold.

"That was fun," I say as we put on our clothes, this time, Justin watches me out of the corner of his eye.

"It was. If only it was warmer out then we could stay in the water longer. Hey, let's go for a walk along the beach."

I smile, liking the idea. Justin puts an arm around my waist and we walk along the shore line in silence. Listening to the waves wash up onto the shore felt relaxing, and I wonder to myself why didn't we ever do something like this before. I imagined doing midnight strolls along the beach with my boyfriend, but it's an opportunity that never really came up. It wasn't something I would expect to be doing with my best friend. But it didn't really matter who I was walking here with. I was just glad that Justin is the one who is here with me.

"Justin?"

"Yeah?"

I turn to look at him with a smile. "I'm glad to have spent the whole night with you."

He returns the smile. "I'm glad to have spent the whole night with you, too."

We stay on the beach a little while longer before fatigue started to take us over. We call for a taxi to take me back to my place. In the backseat of the taxi, I lean against Justin's shoulder, slowly falling asleep. He has this nice scent of cologne that I hadn't taken noticed until now. When the taxi pulls up in front of my house, I almost didn't want to move away from Justin, wanting to keep breathing in his cologne.

Justin walks me to my door. We hesitate there for a moment, neither one of us wanting to say goodbye.

"Thanks for goodnight, Justin."

He smiles. "It's no problem, Amberlee. I'm just really glad I could make you happy tonight."

"Would you like to spend the night here? It's late, and I don't want you to walk the few blocks home."

"Sure. I guess there is no harm in staying the night."

I fumble for my keys in my purse, but I couldn't find it. Justin offers to find it, and as I hand my purse over to him to see if he could locate my keys, his hand brushes slightly against mine. Normally, when our hands brush up against each other it's no big deal. But this time, I felt a tingle. I draw my hand away from him, looking for signs to see if Justin felt what I did. He showed no signs as he pulls out the keys, dangling it in the air.

"Found it! It was right at the bottom underneath everything that you have in there," he says, dramatic and teasing and clearly not feeling what I felt moments before.

He unlocks the door for us, and hands the keys back to me. I take them, thanking him. I switch on the light and walk to the kitchen and put my purse down on the table.

"Hey, would you like a glass of wine?" I ask, reaching for a bottle of red wine from a top cabinet, along with two wine glasses.

"It's late, Am. And don't you think you had enough to drink tonight?"

"Who says we can't have one more?"

I pour the two glasses. Even if Justin didn't say if he wanted more, he takes the glass. He walks out to the lounge room and sits down on the couch. I sit beside him. My knee knocks against his, and there's that slight tingle again. Why was it doing that? My skin never tingles against Justin's touch. It must be the alcohol that is making me feel this.

"So, what are your plans for today?" Justin asks me.

"Well, since I have the day off today, I will probably sleep in. And I really don't want to know about the hangover I will get when I wake up later."

Justin chuckles. "I'm not looking forward to that either."

I watch him down the rest of the drink. I'm pretty sure this was the alcohol talking, but for some reason Justin looked incredibly attractive as he drank the wine. I shake my head. Why am I thinking that my best friend is attractive? I mean, I know he's attractive, but he hasn't been attractive to me in that way. Until tonight.

"Anyway, what do you say we call it a night?" he asks, leaning over to place his empty wine glass on the coffee table. "I feel like I will collapse at any moment. I'll sleep on the couch."

I nod. I drink the rest of my drink and then lean over to put my glass on the table. When I sit up, I lean in closer to Justin.

"Justin, have you ever wondered about us?" The words are out of my mouth before I could even stop myself. I'm sure I was only supposed to think this to myself, but instead I said it out loud. I blush when he looks at me, surprised that I would even say something like this. "I'm sorry. I wasn't supposed to say that out loud."

"What do you mean if I have ever wondered about us?"

I shake my head. "Forget it. It was just a stupid thought in my head, and I don't know why I said it. I think I'm drunk. I will see you in the morning. Goodnight, Justin."

I wrap my arms around him in a hug, and he returns the gesture.

"Are you sure you don't want to talk about what you have

said?" he asks, hands lingering on my arms, holding me gently in place.

I shake my head and pull away. "No, I'm sorry. Forget I even said anything."

I stand up. As I do, Justin reaches out for my wrist. I feel the tingle instantly and my heart races in my chest when I look down at Justin. When did he suddenly become so attractive? We have been best friends for so long so why would I suddenly feel anything for him now? Especially when I've only just broken up with my cheating boyfriend less than forty hours. Isn't this all too soon?

"Goodnight, Amberlee," he says with a small smile and I tell myself I'm imagining the disappointment. "I had fun tonight. You sleep well and I will see you in the morning."

The way he formed his lips into a smile, it gave me this urge to kiss him. Should I kiss him? What will it mean if I did? Will we still be friends?

Chapter Six

I sit back down beside Justin. He doesn't take his eyes off me. We stare at each other for what seems like forever. Are we both sharing the same feeling? Are the feelings real? Or are we too drunk and these feelings are just alcohol and hormones talking?

I reach out and stroke his cheek. I feel his stubble along his jawline as I move my fingers down until I reach the corner of his mouth. Something tells me to kiss him, but I hesitate. What if kissing Justin was the biggest mistake I ever make? It could ruin our friendship. I couldn't lose Justin over a drunken kiss.

I start to move away, but then Justin rests a hand on my jaw. Slowly, he moves forward. I hold my breath as I, too, inch forward until we close the gap between us. The kiss was soft and gentle, just his lips against mine. He pulls away, staring at me. Butterflies circled my stomach. I can't believe this is happening. I can't believe I want this to keep happening.

Justin's face is still close to me, his hands cupped around my jaw and he doesn't seem to move away. I try to tell myself that this was a mistake, but it doesn't seem like we have done anything wrong. In fact, I wanted to kiss him more.

I rest a hand on the back of his neck and kiss him again. He returns the kiss. It's slow at first, but then Justin deepens it. Before I know it, I'm lying on my back with Justin hovering over me. He kisses me down my neck, down my collarbone, and I gasp his name in delight. He murmurs mine against the skin of my neck before claiming my lips again. I couldn't even believe Justin and I were doing this. Of all the nights, why on the early hours of the morning the day after Valentine's Day, did we decide to hook up?

I was feeling things that weren't 'best friend' feelings. They were bigger, more, urgent.

When he breaks away, holding himself above me, I want to let out a noise of complaint, but I manage to hold it in. In jerky movements, Justin pulls away, like he regrets kissing me, or it's suddenly awkward. I sit up beside him, straightening my clothes and hair. I pretend that I don't crave more of him and wonder if he could feel the same.

We sit on the couch, breathless without even looking at each other.

Now that we have crossed this line, where does that leave us?

"I should go to bed," I say, getting off the couch suddenly.

Justin stands. "Yes, we should both go to bed."

"Goodnight, Justin."

I make my way to my room, hoping that maybe Justin will

change his mind about sleeping on the couch, and will join me in my room. I left the door ajar so Justin knew he could come in if he wanted to. Without bothering to change out of my jeans and t-shirt, I lay down on my bed in the dark. I touch my lips and smile. Right now, it doesn't feel like a mistake, and I pray it won't in the morning, either. Once my head hits the pillow, I instantly fall asleep, dreaming about Justin.

Chapter Seven

The sun leaks through my bedroom window. I have no idea what time it is, but I feel more tired than ever and wish I could stay in bed longer. I reach for my phone without sitting up, not wanting to know what kind of hangover I will be facing after the amount of alcohol I had last night. My too bright phone screen tells me it's 8:30.

I groan, and hide my head underneath the pillow. I wonder how Justin feels this morning.

Justin.

Oh my gosh.

I swiftly sit up, instantly regret it as I feel a pounding around my temples. I groan, rubbing my temples. Why on earth did I consume so much alcohol last night?

As I rub my temples, I recall my kiss with Justin. I can't

believe I have kissed my best friend. What was I even thinking last night? Actually, I knew what I was thinking. I was thinking about the way he smelled and felt, and how his shoulder was my favourite place to rest my head. I was not thinking about the fact Justin was my best friend and I was not thinking about what I was risking.

But it made me wonder if Justin had feelings for me, too? Or was the kiss meaningless, a drunken kiss? Wasn't it? But he'd been a pretty active participant, too, so...

Okay, I should think about this later. Right now, I need something for my headache.

I get out of bed and head to the bathroom to take something, downing two tablets. I take a shower to freshen up and then go to see if Justin is up. Only he wasn't sleeping soundly on the couch. Nor was he in the kitchen where I thought he would maybe make breakfast for the both of us. There wasn't even a note or a text message from him to let me know that he was leaving in the morning.

There's this strange feeling in my chest knowing that Justin didn't stay. It's a feeling I have never had before. Is the kiss why Justin isn't here? Did he feel awkward or something to face me after the way we ended last night?

I sit down on the couch, whacking my palm against my forehead. Damn it. Why did I kiss him last night? I should have said no. We had a perfectly good night, one of the best I have either had, and now it may just be ruined because of a stupid kiss.

I pull out my phone and message to let him know I was up, and ask if he wanted to go out for breakfast. Sometimes we go out for breakfast on Sunday when I don't have to work. I stare at my phone, waiting for him to reply back to my message, expecting him to do it in a jiffy, like normal. Like he has the phone right next to him, waiting for my message. But this morning he didn't return it quickly. I wonder if maybe he was still sleeping in, or perhaps he had a hangover so bad that he couldn't get out of bed. My worst fear was he didn't want anything to do with our friendship anymore.

No. Justin would not end our friendship over a kiss, would he? We have been best friends for so long. Why would he suddenly end it over something stupid?

It's all in my head and I need to stop thinking negatively. Justin will text soon, I tell myself. He is probably in the shower or something.

I walk into the kitchen to make myself some toast for breakfast when my phone buzzes with a message. My heart stops beating for a minute as I check to see who has messaged me, but sinks with sadness when it was just my older sister, Alyssa. She asks me if I want to meet up for lunch with her and my one year old nephew, Mickey. I smile and tell her I would love to. It has been a few weeks since I have seen her. She'd been really busy going back to work after a year of maternity leave and I missed her.

And going to lunch will keep my mind off Justin for a while.

* * *

I meet my sister at a café in St. Kilda. Mickey squeals with excitement from his pram when he sees me walking through the door. Alyssa stands up and gives me a hug. Then I turn to my nephew and give him a kiss on his forehead.

"Have you ordered anything yet?" I ask as I take a seat.

"No, I was waiting for you to come before I did."

We look over our menu and order at the counter. I order myself a big breakfast.

"So did you do anything with Rick for Valentine's last night?" I ask.

"We had a nice dinner together. Rick's sister came to look after Mickey for us. It was great because Rick and I don't get many nights alone together."

I smile at her. "Well, I'm happy you had a good night."

"How was your night with Oliver?"

I look away awkwardly. My stomach twists into knots, and suddenly I have no appetite and feel sick for a reason other than my hangover. I was hoping to avoid this question, but I knew I would have to tell my sister eventually. *Everyone* will be talking about their Valentine's dates today.

I adjust the cutlery on the table for something to do with my hands and to avoid looking at her. "Oliver and I broke up on Friday."

Alyssa gasps, and reaches over to take my hand in hers. "Amberlee, I'm so sorry. Why didn't you tell me?"

I shrug. "I don't know why. The very first person I reached out to was Justin. He helped me to feel better. Last night, he invited me to see the Night Rangers, and we spent the entire night together."

Alyssa smiles. "I'm glad to hear that Justin was able to make you feel better. What else did you two do after you finished the concert?"

"We went out for drinks and then hung out at the beach for a bit. Then he took me home and we…"

I end the sentence there, recalling the moment where Justin and I kissed. I still can't decide if the kiss was something we have always wanted to do, or if it was just the alcohol making us do it. But whatever it was, I can't help but feel it was something I wanted to do again.

"What happened, Amberlee?" Alyssa asks me. "Did something happen between the two of you?"

I nod. "We kissed." My voice is small, but when I brave looking up at her, I see that Alyssa is smiling.

"I have always known you and Justin will someday get together."

I look at her. "What?"

She takes a sip of her drink before she answers me. "I have always suspected that you and Justin liked each other more than just friends. You just hadn't been able to see it."

I shake my head. There is no way whatever my sister is saying is true. "Justin and I are just friends. That's all we'll ever be. Besides, I'm sure it will ruin our friendship if we got together."

"Nonsense. Sure, you and Justin can still be friends, but many people do end up marrying their best friends. You've both been in enough relationships that don't go anywhere."

"So what are you saying? That Justin and I are never really going to be happy in a relationship with someone else because we're soul mates?"

Mickey squeals happy in his pram where he is eating a peanut butter sandwich that's cut in squares.

Alyssa nods in his direction.

"See. Even Mickey agrees that you and Justin are perfect for each other."

I let what she was saying to me sink in. I have honestly never really seen Justin as more than a friend. We have been there for each other for so long that I do not know what I would do without him. Last night was probably one of the best nights of my life. We were drunk when we had kissed. Can a kiss still mean something when you're drunk?

I pull out my phone from my purse, a fresh wave of sadness washing over me. It was midday and Justin still hadn't returned my message from this morning. Justin never takes this long to answer back to me. And I wonder if our relationship is doomed now that we have kissed?

I glance up at my sister. "I texted Justin this morning to see if he wanted to go out for breakfast like we would usually do on Sunday mornings, but this time he has ignored my message."

"Did you two have sex last night?" Alyssa asks, leaning forward like a gossip queen.

I stare at her with my mouth sightly opened, mortified. "No! We didn't have sex. We only kissed."

"Good, because having sex would have only made the situation worse."

"What are you talking about?"

"My guess is he's probably thinking about last night and is wondering what he truly feels for you. Or he, as I have long suspected, is terrified you'll laugh it off because he has feelings for you."

"You think he… no, he can't! He'd have said something by now!"

"Amberlee, you aren't great at reading people. But I guarantee that no matter which one of us is right, that boy is scared and confused, just like you."

I nod, understanding where she was coming from. I was beginning to wonder how I truly felt about Justin myself. Normally I'm calmer if he doesn't answer my texts straight away, but today I'm anxious. I feel like tearing out my hair as I wait for him to reply back. What happened last night can't be that bad that he is choosing to ignore me, was it?

Chapter Eight

I message Justin later that afternoon. There was still no answer from him and it was starting to scare me. Justin has *never* ignored me. I think about what my sister had said to me at the café, and I wonder why Justin wasn't answering my text messages. Did he have mixed feelings about us after we had kissed?

Since he wasn't answering my texts, I call him instead. Only it went straight to voicemail – twice!

On the second call, I leave a message.

"Hey, Justin. It's Amberlee. You haven't been answering my texts, and I just want to know if everything is okay with you."

I hang up and sit down on the couch to settle in front of Netflix, in hope it will keep my mind off Justin. But I couldn't concentrate on the rom-com I had chosen to watch. Not when it reminded me of Justin and eating ice cream together while he pretended to care about jocks falling for nerds. Of kissing him and waiting to see what he'd say when we saw each other again...

That's it! I have to see him. There is no use in sitting around waiting for him to call. I have to be the one to make the move. I have to find out why he is avoiding me.

I grab my car keys and headed out the door, driving the few blocks to Justin's. His car is parked out front. He is home. So it wasn't like he was doing something and wasn't getting my messages.

I knock on the front door and was greeted by Justin's mother.

I smile at her. "Good afternoon, Elise. Is Justin home?"

Elise returns the smile. "Hello, Amberlee. It's good to see you. Yes, Justin is just up in his room." She moves aside and lets me enter the house. "How was the concert last night? You had a good time?"

I nod. "Yes, I had a really good time." I had a good time after the concert, too, I don't add. But I think it. Even though I'm going upstairs right now ready to pretend everything is normal if I have to.

She closes the door behind me. "That's good to hear. Go on up. I'm sure Justin will be glad to see you. He has been keeping to himself today. I guess he is just nursing his hangover. Arc you staying for dinner, Amberlee?"

"Yes, I will, thanks." That's if Justin wants me here after we talk.

I run up the stairs and head to Justin's room. I hear the Night Rangers playing on the other side of the door. I stand there for a moment, almost scared to knock. I mean, what if he didn't want to see me?

Get a hold of yourself, Amberlee. Justin is your best friend. He *would* never say he wouldn't want to see you.

I knock on the door.

I hear movement on the other side. The door knob turns and then the door swings open, revealing Justin wearing grey sweat pants and a white tank top.

"Amberlee," he says, surprised to see me.

"Are you avoiding me?" Okay, not the carefully worded question I'd rehearsed on the way over. But desperation took over at the sight of him.

"What? No, I'm not." He scratches his neck – his lying tic.

I push past him into his room and he closes the door behind us. "Don't lie to me, Justin." I spin around to face him. "I have been messaging you all day and you haven't replied. Is this… is this about last night? I'm sorry. I shouldn't have kissed you. It was… a mistake." The words feel like sandpaper in my mouth and Justin flinches. He takes a deep steadying breath and looks me in the eye.

"It wasn't a mistake."

"It wasn't?" My voice is tight in my throat.

He takes a step towards me. "I know I shouldn't have ignored you. I'm sorry. I just… I was trying to process how I felt about the kiss. I just… I was just scared, Am. You were drunk and upset about Oliver and I… I took advantage of you. That was the mistake. The kiss… I'm never going to regret that kiss, Amberlee."

Alyssa was right. Justin wasn't ignoring me. He just needed time to process what was going on between us last night. I'm still trying to figure it out myself, but I know that I don't want to go back. But I'll take whatever he offers because I'm not doing life without him in it. I can't.

"Justin… about last night…"

I try to find the words I wanted to say, but I couldn't find the right ones. I look away from him, unable to face him when I became aware of the butterflies dancing around my stomach. Why haven't I ever felt anything for my best friend before? Is it true what Alyssa said? Are we really meant for each other?

Justin's hand strokes my cheek, making my skin tingle from his touch. He gently lifts my chin so I can't look away.

"Last night was one of the best nights ever," he says. "I know I should have told you why I didn't answer your calls. It was just that I was afraid of my own feelings. I thought avoiding you I would be able to figure out how to pretend that just being your best friend is enough, but the truth is I have been dying to see you all day." He smiles. "And I'm so glad you are here right now."

I return the smile. "So, you aren't mad at me because we kissed?"

He shakes his head, a small laugh escaping. "No. I wanted to kiss you. I've wanted to kiss you since grade nine, Am. Why else would I buy two tickets to a concert on Valentine's Day, just in case you could make it? I don't want to go back to not kissing you. I want… I want you, Amberlee. And if you think this is all a mistake, then… we'll figure it out. But if you think, maybe, that last night could be the start of something different, with me, then I propose we kiss again. Often. Repeatedly."

My smile is so wide it hurts my cheeks, and I tingle with the thrill of pleasure that comes from his words. "Since grade nine, huh?"

"Since grade nine," he repeats, his hand moving to cup my cheek, then stroke down my neck. "You haven't answered my question."

"I would like that very much, Justin Hogan."

"Thank goodness," he says, before he cups his hands around my jaw and kisses me. I don't hesitate to snake my arms around his neck as I return the kiss with equal fervour.

It felt right to be with him like this, and who knew that one whole night could change between us forever.

EVERY MOMENT WITH YOU

<h1 style="text-align:center">Chapter One</h1>

It still feels like some kind of dream I haven't woken up from. But it's the kind of dream I want to keep having repeatedly. Never had I thought I'd get to wake up beside my best friend each day.

It has been three weeks since Valentine's Day – the night Justin and I realised the love we had for each other was more than just friendship. While everyone seemed to have known Justin's feelings for me since Grade Nine, it had taken me four years to realise it. Even though I was heartbroken on Valentine's Day after I caught my boyfriend of five months cheating on me with his ex, I tell myself it was a good thing he did because then I wouldn't have known Justin's true feelings for me.

I replay our first kiss together over and over in my mind, getting butterflies just thinking about it. Justin told me I could blame it all on alcohol, but the kiss felt right – his lips on mine, his body close to me and my arms around his neck as I pull him closer – it was the perfect choice.

In just one night, Justin made me forget I'd been cheated on, made me feel I was important and that I deserved to have a night out on the most romantic day of the year, and not spend it feeling miserable because I was dumped for a much prettier girl the day before. Justin showed me what Oliver was missing out on.

I don't know if it was all too fast since we made our relationship official, but Justin decided to move in with me to help me with rent. It has been a great help now that my ex doesn't live with me. The day he moved in – a week after he started his new marketing job – everything felt right, like it all just fit into place with the two of us together. Not just as friends, but as soulmates. We lived next door to each other for fourteen years, until my older sister got married and I moved out to live with Oliver. With my sister and I gone, our parents decided to downgrade, sold the house next door to Justin's and moved to a small place in St. Kilda.

Now everything feels like old times with us living together, and I love every moment of it.

I watch Justin sleep beside me. He still has a few more minutes before he has to get up to go to work and I start my shift at the coffee shop. I don't know if it makes me look like some kind of creepy person out of a horror film, but I enjoy watching Justin sleep, his face relaxed and peaceful, breathing softly as he lays there. I feel lucky to wake up to someone I know I can always trust and never be let down, unlike the last two relationships I'd been in. And I'm sure Justin feels the exact same way about his own past relationships.

"I know you're watching me, Amberlee," he mumbles in his sleep, his mouth curling into a smile.

I sit up. "What are you talking about?"

His blue eyes sparkle as he sits up. "Don't think I haven't noticed you watching me sleep these last couple of mornings."

"I… I don't know what you're talking about."

My gaze travels down his face to his bare chest. I stare at the little chest hair he has, my eyes wanting to travel down further, but blankets cover his torso.

"Am, I know I'm sexy and that you can't keep your eyes off me," he says with a smirk, "but there is no need for you to watch me. I mean, you could have gotten up and made me breakfast in bed."

I playfully hit his arm. "You could do the same thing for me."

He puts a hand around the back of my neck and the other around my waist, pulling me close to him. "I know. Maybe someday I will surprise you." He strokes the back of my neck. "But for now, come here and give me a kiss."

I gladly lean forward and kiss him, our lips moving slowly against each other as my insides melt from his touch. My body hates me when I pull away and get out of bed.

"I'm going to take a shower," I tell him.

"Yeah?" Justin gives me a cheeky smile. "Do you mind if I join you?"

"No, you pervert." I stick my tongue out at him. "You aren't seeing me naked that easily yet."

"Oh, come on, Am. I have seen you naked before." He climbs out of bed and walks over to me.

My mouth drops open. "Since when?"

"Oh, don't tell me you have forgotten? I definitely haven't. It was my eighteenth and your parents allowed you to come along with my family to Hobart for the long weekend. We snuck out late one night, and because we were staying near the beach you thought it would be fun to go skinny dipping. And I actually thought you were going to do the exact same thing on Valentine's when we visited the beach."

I hide my face so Justin doesn't see how mortified I am. It was fun at the time, but now it's just embarrassing. What the hell was I thinking at that age? It was a wonder Justin didn't want me to strip down when we were drunk on the night of Valentine's. I've always had a wild side that usually Justin only sees, but I'm not sure I would have gone skinny dipping back then if I had known Justin's true feelings for me. I can't imagine what was going through his head when he used to hide his feelings for me.

"I can't believe I made us do that."

He chuckles and removes my hands from my face. "Hey, I wasn't complaining."

"Of course you weren't. But trust me, I'm still not allowing you to hop in the shower with me."

He shrugs. "Well, okay. Maybe it won't be today, but it will be someday." He cups my jaw. "And I swear to you when we decide to go all the way, it will be special."

I smile, the thought of someday sleeping with Justin making my heart do a crazy dance. At the same time, my stomach does a nervous somersault. When Justin and I decided we were going to officially be together, we agreed we weren't going to have sex, not for a while anyway. This whole friends-to-lovers thing was all so new to the both of us, and neither of us wanted to suddenly lose our friendship if nothing worked out. We haven't set a day when we will give it a try, but I guess we will know when it's right.

Justin kisses me one more time and allows me to take my shower.

* * *

It's a busy morning at the café as nearby office workers come in for their coffee fix. Justin works a few blocks away from me and always pops into the café whenever he can. Even though there are other places closer to his office, he says the coffee is better at my workplace. But of course, that's just his way of saying he wants to see me. And I'm glad the office is walking distance to here. I look forward to each day he comes in.

Out of all the people, regulars and non-regulars, who come into the café, I was *not* expecting to see my ex-boyfriend. Out of all the people, regulars and non-regulars, who come into the café, I was *not* expecting to see my ex-boyfriend. I had to do a double-take to really make sure it was him coming through the door. But the boy with dark hair and eyes that walked through was no doubt the guy I had once fallen for.

Oliver had never once stepped foot in the café the whole five months we dated. I can't imagine the reason he chose today to come in.

I give him a small smile to be polite, even though I never want to see his face again. "Oliver, what a surprise. What can I get you?"

"Actually, I was hoping I could talk to you for a second, Amberlee," Oliver says, his dark eyes pleading with me to say yes. He grips a folder at his side.

I'm about to open my mouth to say no. I'm working and I really do not want to speak to him. But before I have the chance to speak, my co-worker Stacey steps in and tells me she will take over so I can see what Oliver wants. I thank her and come out from behind the counter to talk to him.

I fold my arms across my chest. "Okay, you have five minutes to explain what you are doing here."

Oliver inhales a deep breath, letting it go slowly. "I want to start off by saying how sorry I am for sneaking behind your back with Hilary. It's something I should never have done and I'm sorry. It was such a dick thing to do. I want to make it up to you, Amberlee. I miss you and I want us to be together again."

I hear Stacey snicker from the counter. I have to refrain from laughing at Oliver's request. Does he really think I'll take him back after he cheated on me, sneaking around with his then ex-girlfriend for a whole month?

I shake my head, putting my arms at my side. "Nice try, Oliver, but I'm not getting back with you that easy. Not after you betrayed me. Do you have any idea how much it hurt me? I still don't know how to forgive you."

"Hilary and I broke up."

Oh. I get why he is here. He lost his ex and now he thinks he has a chance with me again. Does he really think I'm that stupid after what he did?

"And you think you can just waltz in here and assume I would want to get back with you?"

Oliver glances down at his feet. "It sounded like a good idea when I thought about it. But now when you say it, it sounds awful."

I nod. "It does. I don't want to get back with you after what you did. I'm actually happier than I have ever been since I caught you in bed with your ex. In fact, I'm dating Justin now."

He looks up at the mention of Justin's name, his eyes wide. "Justin? Your best friend Justin?"

I roll my eyes. Like I knew dozens of guys with the name Justin and not just my best friend. "Yes. He helped me to get through the breakup. One thing led to another and now we are dating."

Oliver's face turns from surprised to furious as his eyes narrow at me. "You're seriously dating Justin?"

I nod. "Yes, I am."

He snickers. "I always knew you were banging that guy behind my back."

The way he says it feels like a stab to the heart, like I have been the one cheating on him instead of the other way around.

"Are you saying that I can't have a guy best friend?" I ask him, raising an eyebrow. "Does having a guy best friend mean I'm messing around with him?" I burst into laughter. "Oh, come on, Oliver. You know I would never have cheated on you with Justin, even though I have known him longer than you. He has always been there for me. The day I broke up with you, he was there to get me through it. Without him, I'm pretty sure I wouldn't be in a happy place right now. It doesn't feel like the last five months with you were a complete waste, because the whole time I had Justin to lean on when I needed you."

The smirk he gives me shows that he doesn't believe a word I'm saying.

I fold my arms across my chest. "What are you smirking about?"

"You. I find it so hard to believe that you never did something with that guy."

"Are you assuming I cheated on you with Justin all along?"

I throw my arms in the air. "I'm not a cheater like you, Oliver. And right now I don't have time to talk to you. I should really get back to work. Your five minutes is up."

I turn to leave to get back to work, but Oliver isn't done talking.

"I knew Justin had a thing for you, and not just in a friendship way. That's why I assumed you were messing around with him."

I turn back to him. "Justin wouldn't have made a move on me while I was with you."

He sneers. "Yeah, but I bet he couldn't wait to be all over you once I was out the door."

I rub a hand through my hair. I really don't need to explain my business to my ex. He can think what he wants, but in the end Oliver is the loser. I'm with Justin now and I have no feelings for Oliver.

"Oliver, if you can't speak nicely about Justin, then I suggest you leave. Now excuse me, but some of us need to work."

I walk around to the counter when Oliver speaks again.

"I have something for you," he says, waving the folder in his hand.

I take the manila folder and see my name on it in his messy handwriting. I open it up to find booking details for a hotel in the Yarra Valley. I look up at him. "What is this?"

"This was supposed to be your birthday present," Oliver explains. "I booked it just before you found me with Hilary. Your birthday is next week and I wanted to give this to you. I was hoping we could still go together, but maybe you and Justin will benefit instead."

If I hadn't broken up with him, I would have jumped for joy and kissed him right on the spot for booking this getaway.

But I keep my cool as I thank him for still allowing me to have this getaway. He could have told me to forget about it and gone on the trip himself, but instead he let me have this trip I could enjoy with Justin.

Without another word, Oliver leaves the café, walking out of my life for good.

Chapter Two

"You will never guess who showed up at the café today," I tell Justin once my shift ends for the day. After work he always meets me outside the café, and I always have a coffee ready for him to drink on our commute home.

"Yeah?" Justin asks as we cross the road to the tram station. I didn't have to mention his name for Justin to know exactly who I was talking about. "What did that douchebag want?"

"Can you believe he came in and asked me to take him back?"

He stops in the middle of the road, staring at me with a mixture of surprise and fear, like maybe I was considering going back to Oliver. A car beeps at him, making him jump and bringing him back to reality. We cross the rest of the way until our feet are on the kerb of the tram stop.

"You're joshing, right?" he asks me once we're safe on the kerb.

"I wish I was." I stand close to him in the crowded tram stop. "Apparently, he only wanted to get back with me because the girl he cheated on me with dumped him."

Justin chuckles. "Karma." He looks at me, face becoming serious. "So, what did you say?"

"I told him I wasn't interested and that I was with you. He wasn't very happy." I leave out the part where Oliver said he knew about Justin liking me. I don't want him to feel he was the cause of the breakup, because he wasn't. I'm thankful for walking in on Oliver because then I wouldn't have known about how Justin felt towards me.

Justin smiles and puts his arms around me. "Well, that's what he gets for messing around with another woman and not seeing that the perfect woman is standing right here. He could have had you for the rest of his life, but he chose not to."

I blush at his comment. "I'm not that perfect."

"To me you are." He removes his arm from around me, brushing his hand gently across my cheek before leaning in and kissing me softly.

He pulls away just as the tram arrives. He takes my hand and we board, leading us towards two empty seats at the back. I sit down near the window while he sits in the aisle seat.

"So, do you have any plans for my birthday next weekend?" I ask.

Justin sets his messenger bag on his lap. He holds his coffee cup in his left hand and puts his other arm around my shoulders. He thinks for a moment. "Your birthday? No, I have nothing planned."

The bell dings as the doors close, and the tram begins

moving. Justin takes a sip of his coffee, avoiding my eyes.

"Liar," I say, curling my lips into a smile. "You do have plans."

He downs the rest of his coffee. Still not meeting my eyes because he knows I will see straight through him, he says, "You know something? I'm glad I'm dating you because you make the best coffee in the whole of Melbourne."

I slap his chest playfully. "Don't change the subject. You aren't getting out of this conversation that easily."

He turns to me with a smile. "If I tell you my plans then it wouldn't be a surprise."

"A surprise, huh? Well, I can wait for it."

"Good, because you will have to and I'm not leaving you any hints." He leans over and gives me a quick kiss.

The tram slows to a stop, opening the doors for passengers to get on or off.

"Whatever surprise you have for me, there is something else we can do for my birthday."

"Oh yeah? What's that?"

"You know how I told you Oliver came in today, wanting to get back with me?"

"Yeah." His jaw clenches at the mention of Oliver.

"Well, he told me he booked a getaway for my birthday before I caught him with his ex. He was hoping I would get back with him so we could go together, but when I told him I'm happy with you he decided to let me take the trip with you. How does the Yarra Valley sound next weekend?"

The bell dings as the doors close and the tram begins moving once again.

"Sweet. I can't say no to a getaway in the Yarra Valley. It will be a perfect trip."

I smile. "I can't wait."

* * *

Once home, I sit down at the kitchen table while Justin prepares dinner. I enjoy it when he allows me to take breaks from cooking. I never got that opportunity with Oliver. He didn't like cooking. Tonight it's Justin's turn. I have no idea what he's preparing, something with chicken, but the smell makes my stomach grumble.

I read over the papers Oliver gave me, curious to know what kind of trip he had planned. He had booked us a lodge in a winery, along with a wine and cheese tasting tour. The next day he had organised a hot air balloon ride. After that, we had free time for ourselves to do whatever we wanted before we booked out of our accommodation.

"Wow," I say.

Justin looks over his shoulder as he stirs fettuccine in a pot. "What is it?"

"Okay, so despite Oliver being a jerk, he has set up a really nice trip," I say. "We will be staying at lodge at a winery, where we'll do a wine tasting tour. And in the morning before we leave, we are going on a hot air balloon ride."

Justin's face goes pale. "A hot air balloon ride?"

I get off the chair and rest a hand on Justin's cheek. "Hey, it will be alright. I will be there with you, so you don't have to feel scared."

He nods. "I know, but I don't know if I can do it. It's bad enough I have to work in an office building without feeling vertigo whenever I look out the window."

"I promise you will be fine once we reach the sky. You will

want to admire the beauty of the valley, not worry about how far up we are."

"Of course not." He turns back to the stove, stirring the pasta.

"How's the cooking coming along?" I ask.

"Good. I should be almost done."

"Great. I'm starving."

I stand beside him to watch him cook.

"My mum contacted me today," Justin says. "She wants to know if you would like to come over for dinner tomorrow night."

"I would love to. I don't think I have seen your parents since I helped you move. We have to make a day for them to come visit. And don't forget that my parents, along with my sister and her husband, are coming for dinner on Saturday."

"I haven't forgotten, and I definitely agree we need to invite my parents over next time. They would honestly love this place. Hey, dinner is almost ready. Do you want to start setting the table?"

"Sure." I give him a peck on the cheek and go to set the table.

I take out the placemats and spread them out on the table, glancing over at Justin. He takes a piece of the pasta out and tastes it. Satisfied with how it was cooked, he takes the pot off the stove and places it in a strainer over the sink. I watch him carefully, wondering if he's really okay with the whole trip Oliver had planned out. He was quick to change the subject and didn't ask me anymore questions about it, or any other activities we could do. Did he have a lot on his mind about the hot air balloon ride, wondering how he would overcome his fear?

Or maybe it wasn't about his fear. Maybe it was about Oliver showing up out of nowhere. I really hope this trip will not be a problem at all just because my ex had planned it. I wanted this trip to be about the both of us, and not about someone who is no longer a part of my life.

65

Chapter Three

After work, before we take the tram home, Justin and I stop by the supermarket to grab flowers for his mum. Elise loves lilies, so I buy her a bouquet of pink ones. Of course, I didn't need to get her any, but it was the first dinner Justin and I were attending with his parents since he moved out so I felt it was nice to get some flowers. I also get a box of chocolates.

Justin and I head home to get ready, then drive the few blocks to his parents' home.

Elise greets us as soon as we arrive. She pulls her son into a tight hug before turning to me.

I hand her the flowers and chocolate. "These are for you, Elise."

Elise takes the gift from me. "Oh, thank you, Amberlee. They are lovely."

Justin's dad, Darren, joins us at the front door. "It's good to see you two."

He hugs his son before giving me one too. Elise closes the door and tells us to make our way to the kitchen and sit down. Dinner was almost ready. I sit next to Justin at the four-seater table. Darren sits across from him while Elise finishes preparing the food.

"So how do you two find it living together?" Darren asks us.

"We really enjoy each other's company," Justin says. "I don't think we have much of a problem living together. Maybe it's because we've known each other for so long, but we get along very well under the same roof."

"That's great to hear," Elise says, walking over to us carrying two plates. She places one down in front of Justin and the other in front of me.

"Do you need any help, honey?" Darren asks, starting to rise from his chair, but she only tells him to stay seated. He listens to her. It's for the best; I don't want to ruin Elise's good mood. When she's in the kitchen, you stay out of the kitchen.

Elise grabs the other two plates and sets them down. We say a quick prayer and then dig into the delicious grilled chicken with mashed potato and green beans.

"I'm not surprised you two enjoy living together," Elise says. "I remember as kids you didn't want to leave to go back to your own houses when you had sleepovers."

Justin chuckles as he takes a sip of his drink. "Well, now it's like a permanent sleepover." He places his glass down and goes back to eating.

"I don't know why we never gave this dating thing a go earlier," I say.

Justin nods. "We could have. But you were too oblivious to see I had feelings for you."

I let out a sigh as I chew a piece of chicken. Everyone liked to remind me of that, how they all knew Justin liked me, but it wasn't something I took notice of before. If the breakup with Oliver never happened, I may not have discovered Justin's feelings for me. I didn't catch feelings for him until I was drunk, wanting to forget about Oliver as I spent Valentine's with my best friend. I wanted to blame the kiss on the alcohol, believing it was a line we shouldn't have crossed as friends, but Justin told me that even if I blamed it all on being drunk, his feelings for me were real.

And the kiss was the best thing that ever happened to us.

"Yes, I know I have been oblivious, but it doesn't matter now because we are together," I say once I finish chewing my food.

"Do you two have any plans for the future together?" Elise asks as she cuts into her chicken.

"Mum!" Justin says.

Elise looks innocently at him. "What? It's just a question."

"Well, it's still too early to know what our future plans are," I explain. "I mean, it has only been three weeks since we started dating. It's still pretty new to us."

"Of course it is," Darren says with a smile. "It will take time, but one day being a couple will just be second nature to you."

I nod in agreement. "Definitely. I think it will be easier for us, too, since we have known each other for so long."

"The only plan we have made so far is what we are going to do next weekend for Amberlee's birthday," Justin explains. "Other than that, we have nothing planned for the future. Not yet anyway."

"Oh." Elise smiles. "Yes, I almost forgot it was your birthday. What are your plans? Are you doing anything special for your twentieth?"

I smile, reaching for my drink, taking a sip before I speak. "We are going to Yarra Valley."

"Yarra Valley?" Elise looks surprised. She turns to Justin, eyebrows raised. "I thought you said –"

"I am," Justin says quickly. "Yarra Valley was the place Amberlee's *ex* was going to take her for her birthday." He says ex like the word is poison. "He was nice enough to allow Amberlee to take the trip with me."

Elise turns to me with a smile. "That sounds really nice. What will you two be doing there?"

I look between Elise and Justin, who doesn't meet my eyes, wondering what she was going to say before Justin cut her off. I turn back to her and Darren, talking about what the weekend will be like.

Darren laughs at the part about taking a hot air balloon ride. "You are going to have a hard time getting Justin to go on the balloon."

Justin chuckles awkwardly, not wanting any of the attention on him.

"I know, but I told him that I will be there for him at all times," I say.

"Well, I'm sure it will be a wonderful birthday for you, Amberlee," Elise says. "So, how are your parents? I haven't spoken to your mother for a while."

I nod, swallowing some mashed potato before answering. "They are good. They went on a cruise to New Zealand over the weekend. They will be gone for two weeks."

"Oh, that's excellent. I hope they enjoy their time."

"I'm sure they will. They have been planning this trip for a whole year."

We continue talking and eating, and I'm glad the conversation has moved away from how Justin and I are doing together. Justin talks about his new job and how much he loves it. They ask about my studies too, where I'm studying to be a marine biologist while I work.

"I really enjoyed the dinner tonight," I say to Justin once we're in the car. We wave goodbye to his parents who wave back from the front lawn of their house.

Justin honks the horn at them and pulls away from the kerb. "It was a good dinner. It takes me back to the days when you used to stay for dinner so you had an excuse to not go home."

"Yes, I remember those days," I answer with a huge smile on my face.

My mind wanders to Elise looking to Justin for answers when I said we were going to Yarra Valley. "Hey, you know when your mum looked surprised we were going to Yarra Valley for my birthday, but you cut her off… What was she going to ask you?"

Justin keeps his eyes on the road, slowing down at a T-intersection. He looks both ways. "Oh, it was nothing."

"It didn't look like it was nothing. Did you have something planned for me?"

"Maybe, but I have to try and work it in with Oliver's gift."

"What are you planning? We can still do it before we go to Yarra Valley."

Justin turns left at the intersection. "We are, but it's all a surprise so you will have to wait until your birthday on Saturday."

I smile. "Well, I can't wait to see what you have gotten me."

Chapter Four

Wednesdays I have the house to myself while Justin goes off to work. I work on an assignment for my online course. I get as much done as I possibly can before catching a tram into the CBD, where I meet up with Justin for lunch. It's something we started doing on Wednesdays on my day off once he had gotten the marketing job.

When I get home from lunch, I work on more assignments before cleaning up the house. It's my sister Alyssa's wedding anniversary today and I'm babysitting my nephew Mickey tonight. I make sure everything I don't want my nephew to touch is put away. He has started grabbing furniture to pull himself up and stand. He started crawling a couple of months ago. Alyssa is sure he'll be walking soon. I already told Justin we had to have our eyes everywhere to make sure Mickey doesn't get himself in any trouble.

Alyssa shows up to my house at five-thirty with Mickey in her arms.

I spread my arms wide at the sight of my nephew. "Mickey!"

He squeals with happiness, holding his arms out to me. I take him from my sister.

"Thank you so much for taking care of him tonight, Amberlee," Alyssa says as I move aside for her and she slips into the house.

I give her a small smile. "It's no problem, Alyssa." I hold Mickey's hand. "Mickey is going to have a great night with Aunty Amberlee." I look back up at my sister. "You have a great night with Rick."

Alyssa walks over to the coffee table and sets down Mickey's bag. She turns to me. "I'm not sure what time we will finish our date."

"Hey, it's okay. Even if you and Rick want the whole night to yourself, go ahead. I will have Mickey ready for you when you pick him up in the morning before you take him to day care."

"Oh, Am. I don't want to be a pain and make you take care of Mickey all night."

"Alyssa, it's your anniversary. Go and have a great night with Rick. Get all of the alone time you need. Mickey will be fine with Justin and me tonight."

My sister smiles brightly at me. "Thank you, Amberlee. You don't know how much that means to me." She turns to Mickey. "See you later, sweetie. You be good for Aunty Amberlee and Justin, I will see you in the morning." She kisses Mickey's cheek and he squeals.

Alyssa says goodbye to me and heads out the door.

I turn to my nephew. "Do you want to help me finish cooking dinner? Justin should be home soon."

Mickey squeals in answer. Resting him on my hip, I walk over to his bag and swing it over my shoulder. I set him down in the highchair in the kitchen. I take out the blue teddy bear I brought him when he was born and give it to him to play with, hoping the bear is enough to keep him entertained until I finish dinner.

The timer on the oven goes off and I walk over to check on the homemade pepperoni pizza. I turn off the oven and keep the pizza warm inside until Justin comes home. In the meantime, I finish putting together the salad and get dinner ready for Mickey. I move his highchair closer to the table and place his bib around him. I open the baby food Alyssa packed and place it in a bowl to warm it up in the microwave.

The front door opens just as I sit down to feed Mickey.

"Amberlee?" Justin calls out.

"In the kitchen!" I call back.

I dip the spoon in the food and lift it up to Mickey's mouth. He gladly takes the pasta, the Bolognese sauce getting on his chin and around his mouth.

Justin walks in, making his way over to me and kisses me on the cheek. "How was your day?"

"It has been great. Yours?"

He shrugs. "It has been a long day and I'm just glad to be home."

Mickey lets out a small cry and I realise I have been too busy talking to my boyfriend rather than giving him more food. I apologise and give him another spoonful of macaroni. Mickey's face lights up as he chews.

Justin chuckles when he sees my nephew's face covered

with sauce. "That's delicious, isn't it, mate?" Justin says to Mickey.

Mickey doesn't respond, too focused on eating another spoonful of macaroni.

"I will get dinner plated up while you feed Mickey," he says, making his way to the oven.

"Thanks, babe."

Justin takes the pizza out of the oven. "Oh, yum, my favourite."

I glance over at him to see a huge grin on his face as he grabs the cutter and begins cutting the pizza into slices.

"Mickey, when you grow up, you are going to love your aunt's cooking," Justin says. "Especially her homemade pizzas."

I wait for Mickey to say something in response, but the macaroni was all he cared about at the moment as he happily chewed his food.

"I think you will need to have this conversation with him when he is a bit older," I tell Justin. "Right now he doesn't care about anything except for his food."

Justin just laughs and takes the pizza pan to the table, along with two plates for us and the salad bowl. He pours us each a glass of Coke.

I finish up Mickey's dinner and then sit down with Justin to eat. He talks about how the rest of his day went after I last saw him at lunch. When he finishes dinner, he tells me to go take care of Mickey while he cleans the dishes.

I take Mickey to the bathroom to start getting him ready for bed. I had set up a portable cot in the spare room for whenever I had my nephew over. I fill up his toddler bath and put him in it.

Once his bath is over, I wrap him in a towel and then take

him to the spare room. Since he wasn't meant to be sleeping over tonight, Alyssa hadn't packed his pyjamas. I put on a clean outfit she had packed, as his other outfit somehow managed to get sauce on it even though he had a bib on.

Mickey's bedtime is around seven o'clock, and he has another fifteen minutes. He doesn't seem sleepy at all, so I sit down on the guest bed, resting my back against the pillows with Mickey on my lap, and read a bedtime story to him. He listens excitedly as I read the story out to him, pointing to the pictures and telling him what was happening. He claps when something good happens in the story and grabs at the book, but I make sure he doesn't rip the pages.

Towards the end of the book, he starts to get sleepy, so I put him down in the portable cot. Justin stands at the door, watching me. I didn't even know he was there as I read my nephew to sleep. He had changed out of his suit, now dressed in grey track suit pants and a Night Ranger t-shirt. I gesture him to be quiet as I switch off the light to the bedroom and close the door.

"Have I ever told you that how great you are with your nephew?" Justin says with a grin.

"Nope, never," I answer.

"Well, I'm telling you now." He places his hands on my hips and moves me closer to him. "It makes me wonder what you will be like with our own kids someday."

I smile at him. "Thanks. I try to be the best aunt I can be with Mickey."

"And you will make an excellent mother someday. Seeing you with Mickey makes me glad that I finally took a chance on you to be the love of my life."

My heart flutters. "Thanks, Justin. That really means a lot."

I take his hands into mine. "So now that I have gotten Mickey asleep, what do you want to do tonight? We can snuggle on the couch and watch something on Netflix. I told Alyssa not to worry about coming to pick up Mickey tonight like she was planning to do, so she is coming in the morning."

He gives me another flirty grin. "Excellent. That means I have you all to myself."

Without warning, he lifts me up and I wrap my legs around his waist.

"What are you doing?" I ask as I wrap my arms around his neck.

He doesn't answer as he presses his lips against mine. He moves us to our room. He pulls apart for a second to switch on the light. He kisses me again before placing me gently on the bed. Justin climbs on top of me and starts nibbling on my neck.

I gasp. "You are in an extremely good mood tonight."

"I always am when I'm with you."

"We aren't having sex tonight if that's what you are hoping."

He kisses the side of my jaw while he rests his hand on the other side. "I can only hope."

I grab his hand and turn to face him. "I know, and we will someday. We may have known each other for a long time, but this whole dating scene with you is all new to me. I want to be sure that this is where we want to be, and not feel that this is all a mistake and ruin everything between us."

Justin shakes his head, getting off me and leaning his elbow on the bed as he rests his head on his hand. "Trust me, Am, but this is not a mistake. I used to tell myself it would be a mistake when I first started getting feelings for you. When you asked me to be your date at your sister's wedding, I kept wondering to myself what our life would look like together if I wasn't too much of a wimp to ask you out. I have been in love with you for so long that I can't imagine being with anyone else."

I smile at him, knowing that everything he said was true. I still remember the first time I saw him out on the front lawn of his house when we were four, watching as my family moved in next door while he played with his toy truck, his father doing the gardening. I made the first move, getting out of the car and skipping over to their property rather than walking inside the house with my parents and sister. My mum ran after me to make sure I wasn't going to run off.

"I'm Amberlee," I proudly told him with a smile as I stuck out my hand. "Do you want to be friends?"

It was the start of our friendship and we had been inseparable since then. When I first made the decision to move in with Oliver, it was the most difficult choice I ever made. But with Justin, it was a decision I didn't have to take time to think about. I have been around him for so long that I can't imagine my life without him. And now it felt right to have him here with me.

"So, are you still up to snuggling on the couch watching Netflix?" Justin asks me.

I nod with a smile. "Let's do so before Mickey has any plans of waking up."

Chapter Five

The rest of the week went by pretty quickly and my weekend getaway with Justin was here.

I woke to the smell of waffles coming from the kitchen. I usually wake up before Justin, but today he was up early. I walk into the kitchen to find him adding chocolate sauce over a four-layer waffle cake, with cream cheese in between the layers. I remember for my fifth birthday Justin wanted to do something special, as it was the first one we were celebrating together. He made a waffle cake with the help of his mum. Every now and again he liked to make a waffle birthday cake for me. I have made one for him occasionally, but usually I like to get an actual cake for him.

"Mmm, the waffles smell good," I say.

Justin looks up at me, surprised to see me awake, almost

dropping the saucepan of chocolate sauce. "Amberlee! You weren't supposed to come into the kitchen yet."

"Oh. I'm sorry, Justin. I just smelt the waffles and came in here."

"That's okay." He finishes pouring the sauce and places the pan on the table. He then comes over and kisses me softly. "Happy birthday, Am."

"Thanks, Justin," I say as I pull away.

"But seriously, you shouldn't be in the kitchen. I'm not finished with the cake yet. Go and have a shower, freshen up. When you're done, we can sit down to breakfast."

I do as he says so he can get back to making the waffle cake.

I spend at least half an hour getting ready, hoping that will give Justin the time he needs to treat me to the breakfast surprise I ruined for myself. I put on a knee-length blue dress with spaghetti straps, sunflowers decorated on it. I bought it a week ago to wear for my birthday. I throw a denim jacket over it. I'm finishing my make-up when Justin knocks on the door.

He stares at me, taking the dress in. "Wow. You look really nice."

I put my mascara down on the dressing table. "Thanks." I spin around so he can get a full glimpse of what I'm wearing. "I bought it for today."

"Yeah, about that…" He rubs his hand behind his neck. "I don't think you should wear that today."

I stare at him. He was joking, right? "What do you mean I shouldn't wear it? What's wrong with it?"

"Nothing!" he says. "You can still wear it, but wear it when we go to the valley. Sorry, I should have told you what to wear, but I was busy making sure the cake was perfect. The place I'm taking you for your surprise requires you to wear something warm. So maybe you can put on a pair of jeans."

I nod. "Yeah, sure. Okay. Where are we going?"

Justin smiles brightly. "It's a surprise."

"Oh, come on. How am I supposed to know what to wear if you don't tell me where we are going?"

"Trust me. You will want to wear something warm for this. And I promise you that you will like this surprise."

"Okay. I will go change."

He takes my hand. "Later. Come on out and have some breakfast."

I follow him out to the kitchen. As we get closer to the kitchen, he covers my eyes.

"Surprise!" he says, removing his hands.

In the centre of the table is the waffle cake I had walked in on him making. It was now finished, mixed berries on top of the chocolate sauce, dusted with sugar. Sticking out on top were two and zero candles for twenty. The fire flickered, waiting for me to blow it out.

"Happy birthday, Amberlee."

I spin around and wrap my arms around Justin's neck. "Thank you, Justin."

"You're more than welcome." He kisses me just as the doorbell rings.

He lets me go and I go to get the door, knowing who it is before I even answer. Alyssa said she would be coming over with her husband and Mickey. My parents were away on their cruise, but it didn't worry me they weren't able to come.

I open the door and find Alyssa balancing Mickey on her hip, holding two golden balloons in the shape of the number twenty. Mickey was eyeing the balloons, trying to reach for them, but Alyssa kept moving them away from him.

"Happy birthday, Amberlee," she says.

I move aside so she can come in. Her husband Rick walks in behind her, holding a small gift in his hand. "Happy birthday, Amberlee," he says, wrapping me into a hug.

"Thanks for coming, Rick."

"No problem." He hands me the gift. "Here. This is something from Alyssa and I. Well, Alyssa really. I wasn't sure what to get you, so your sister added my name to the card."

"That's okay. I'm just happy to have you here."

I close the door and walk them to the kitchen. Justin takes the balloons from my sister so she can put Mickey in the highchair. Justin ties the strings to a chair. Mickey is getting upset because he wanted the balloons.

I kneel in front of him. "Hey, buddy. The balloons are really for me, but how about when the party is over, I will let you keep one of them?"

He stares at me blankly for a few seconds before smiling brightly.

"Okay, Birthday Girl," Justin says. "It's time to blow out the candles."

We stand at the table, everyone singing happy birthday to me. I then blow out the candles. I take off the candles and cut a slice of waffle cake for everyone. Alyssa gives Mickey some of the berries.

"So, what are you two lovebirds doing today?" Rick wants to know, taking a bite of cake.

"Well, after this I'm taking Amberlee out to the surprise I have for her," Justin explains. "And then later we are going to the Yarra Valley for the weekend."

"Oh, that will be nice," Alyssa says.

"Yeah, the trip was unexpected. It was actually a birthday

gift Oliver had planned for Amberlee, but he allowed us to take the trip together."

"Well, I hope you enjoy your time." Alyssa turns to me with a smile. "I really hope you like the surprise Justin has for you."

"Do you know what it is?" I ask.

Instead of answering my question, she picks up the gift that I had placed on the table. "Why don't you open up your present?"

I open the present. Inside was a personalised sister mug of Alyssa and I as a cartoon, with a quote about what being a sister was about. I smile at it. I remember getting my sister one like this for Christmas, and she was now returning the favour. "Thank you, Alyssa," I say. "It's great."

We finish up breakfast before my sister and her husband leave with Mickey so Justin could take me to my surprise.

Chapter Six

Justin and I catch the tram to Batman Park. Once we cross the road safely from the tram stop, Justin takes off a black bandana he had tied around his neck.

"Ready for your surprise?" he says with a smile.

"I'm ready. So what is my surprise?"

"Patience, Birthday Girl. You will know in just a moment. But first I need you to put this blindfold on." He holds the bandana up and then stands behind me, covering my eyes and tying it behind my head.

"Why do I get the feeling that you're about to surprise me with the best gift ever?" I ask.

I hear Justin moving and then feel his hands cupping either side of my jaw.

"It may be," he says. "I just know that what I'm about to

give you is something you have been wanting for a very long time." He removes his hands from my face and takes my left hand in his. "Are you ready for your surprise now?"

I bounce excitedly. "Of course I am! Come on, Justin. Quit stalling and show me what it is."

He chuckles. "Okay. Just keep holding my hand and I will guide you along."

Justin leads the way. I follow him, coming up with a million things in my head that he could be surprising me with. Maybe he was taking me to a restaurant or something. We are beside the river and I wonder if we're going to the restaurant that we had gone to on Valentine's Day.

We walk along the grass until our feet hit the pavement. Around me I can hear the traffic, the ducks beside the river (or maybe they were swans?). I hear other people in the park also. A train goes by on the tracks next to us and a tram's bell sounds nearby.

"Are we almost there?" I ask as we come to a stop.

"Almost. Are you doing okay?"

I nod. "I just can't wait to take this blindfold off so I can see where you are taking me."

"Just a few more minutes and you can take it off."

I hear the sound of the crossing at the lights and Justin begins moving again, pulling me along. We walk a bit further until we stop and he starts untying the bandana.

"Ready?" he asks me.

I nod. "Ready."

The blindfold comes off and I see the Melbourne Aquarium in front of me.

I turn to Justin, who has a great big grin plastered on his face. "The aquarium?"

He nods. "It's part of the surprise." He pulls out something that looks like passes from the top pocket of his denim jacket. "This is your surprise. Happy birthday, Amberlee."

I take the tickets from him. Two passes for the penguin enclosure experience. Being able to get up close to the King and Gentoo penguins was a dream come true. I have wanted to visit the aquarium to see them, but I never expected to have the opportunity to go into their enclosure.

I squeal with happiness, flinging my arms around Justin's neck. "I love you, I love you!" I give him a quick peck. "Thank you so much, Justin."

He returns a smile. "You are welcome, Am. I knew you wanted to see them for a long time, so I saved up to get us both tickets for it."

Taking my hand, Justin and I enter the building.

* * *

We're taken through to see the food preparation and veterinary areas before stepping onto the ice in the penguin enclosure. I have to refrain from running over to them and scooping them into a hug.

Our tour guide, Cindy, tells us about some of their penguins and some facts that I already knew, but I listen carefully to what she has to say.

Justin and I kneel on the ice, glancing around the enclosure, admiring the birds. Some of the Gentoos were swimming around in the water, while the Kings stood on the ice, either alone or with their partners.

A King wanders over to Justin and I.

"Hello," I say to it. "How are you?"

Justin chuckles. "It's not going to talk back, Am."

I bump him gently. He almost falls, but manages to steady himself.

I open my arms for a hug even though I know I'm not getting one from the penguin. "You are just so cute, you know that? I really want to give you a hug."

As though the penguin knew what I was talking about, it spread its flippers. Or maybe it was just imitating me.

"I think this penguin wants to give you a hug in return," Justin tells me.

"And I really wish I could, but I'm not allowed to."

We stay with the penguins for a bit longer before our time is up. I really wish I could stay longer here.

"I can't wait to get my degree in marine biology," I say to Justin as we walk hand-in-hand into the gift shop. "I hope to be able to work with penguins someday."

"You will, and I'm pretty sure they would enjoy working with you, too. That penguin that came up to you who looked like it wanted to give you a hug surely liked you."

Justin stops in front of a shelf full off a plushies and pulls off a baby King penguin. He holds it up in front of him. In a playful voice he says, "I love you, Amberlee, but Justin loves you more."

I laugh at his childish playfulness. "You aren't jealous that the penguin may like me?"

"No, of course not."

He takes the plush toy and walks over to the register to buy it. Once outside, he hands it to me.

"Here, to always remember your experience up close with your favourite animal," Justin says. I take it from him. "Happy birthday, Am."

I hug him tightly. "Thank you, Justin. This was the best present ever." I peck his lips, pulling away and snuggling the plush toy.

Justin smiles brightly. "I'm so glad you enjoyed yourself. So, should we head home and drive out to the Yarra Valley?"

I take his hand. "Definitely."

Chapter Seven

The lodge Oliver had booked was beautiful, right beside a winery. I was glad that even though he was disappointed I was with Justin now, he still allowed me to have an opportunity to come here for the birthday he had planned.

Justin and I walk into our room on the ground floor, which had a garden view. I stand at the sliding glass door, peering outside, feeling lucky to be here with Justin. He walks up behind me and puts his arms around my waist, resting his chin on my head.

"What time is the wine tasting tour?" he asks.

"It's at three o'clock."

He pulls out his phone to have a look at the time. "We should get going so we won't be late."

We set our bags down and get ready to head out to the

winery nearby.

Justin and I wander around the vineyard with our guide as he talks about the process of making wine, before giving us a behind-the-scenes look at how it's made. Once we finish seeing how it's all made, we finally get to my favourite part of the tour: tasting the wines, along with trying some of the cheeses. Wine isn't one of Justin's favourite beverages, as margaritas are more of his thing. But he likes to sip one every now and then, especially when I offer him some.

After the tour we head back to the lodge and get dinner at the restaurant there. First off, I decide to change out of the jeans I wore to the aquarium and put on the dress I was originally going to wear today. It had gotten cooler by the evening, so I put my denim jacket over it.

"What did you think of the wine tasting tour?" I ask Justin once we're settled in the restaurant and had ordered our food.

"I quite enjoyed it. I had always thought it would be boring considering I'm not much of a wine fan, but I really enjoyed seeing how the wine is made."

"Same here."

"You look really beautiful in that dress."

I look down at the dress and smile. "Thanks. Maybe I couldn't wear it the entire day like I planned to, but at least this dress fits perfectly well for tonight."

"I agree."

The waitress returns with our drinks – a beer for Justin and a red wine for me.

"What do you want to do tonight?" Justin asks. "I'm not sure if there are any night events here, but maybe we could order room service and watch something on TV."

I take a sip of my drink and nod. "Mmm, room service

sounds good. I'm definitely up for that."

Justin smiles. "Great. Well, once we finish up here, we can head back to our room."

* * *

I wanted more wine, but after two glasses Justin cuts me off. He doesn't always stop me from having more, but he knows how wild I can get when I'm a little tipsy. And I guess the wine tasting was probably enough on top of the two glasses I had for dinner.

He kicks back his shoes and sits on the foot of the bed. I join him.

"So what time is the hot air balloon ride tomorrow?" he asks me.

"We need to be at the meeting place at four-thirty."

"Oh wow. Well, I guess we should maybe skip staying up to watch TV and get an early night."

I nod. "You're probably right. We don't have to go to bed just yet. Let's order dessert from room service first."

"Definitely. I feel like a sundae."

I get off the bed and walk over to where the TV stand is. There is a blue folder that has a list of information on the hotel. I flip through the folder until I come to the room service menu, scanning the page.

"Hey, will you be mad at me if I suddenly couldn't go on the hot air balloon with you?" Justin asks me. "I know Oliver booked this tour for the both of you and you aren't afraid of heights. But I'm not sure how I will be tomorrow, and just thinking about it, I don't think I can go through with it."

I glance up from the book, seeing the worry in his eyes.

"Justin, no." I close the folder and put it back down on the TV stand, walking over to my boyfriend. "I have known you almost my whole life, and I can't be mad at you for being afraid of heights." I stand in front of him. "But I would love it if you could put your fear aside and join me in the balloon. If you can't, I won't be mad."

Justin smiles and puts his hands on my waist, pulling me closer to him. "Thanks, Am. I will try not to disappoint you."

I rest a hand on his cheek. "You can do it, Justin. If you can work on the sixth floor of a building, I'm sure you can handle a hot air balloon."

He nods. "You're right, although I think that's a totally different thing."

"Maybe." I sit on his lap. "You will do fine, Justin. I will be right there with you."

I press my lips against his and wrap my arms around his neck. Justin moves his hands to my waist and his lips down to my neck. He finds my sweet spot and I softly moan. I pull away for a second, seeing the lust in Justin's eyes. I know what he wants, but I just don't feel ready yet. I press my lips against his again, pushing him gently down on the bed. He flips us over so he's on top of me, deepening our kiss.

Justin pulls away, stroking my cheek. "So, you still want to order room service?"

I smile at him, pushing him off me and getting up from the bed, and grab the blue folder from the TV stand.

Chapter Eight

Justin doesn't start freaking out about the hot air balloon ride until we are about to get into the basket. Although he had promised me he would give it a go despite his fear of heights, he seemed to have changed his mind once he caught sight of the balloon, reality suddenly hitting him.

His body begins to shake, and I know if I don't get Justin to control his fear, there's no way either of us will be going on this balloon ride. Justin would just tell me to go on my own and enjoy the view without him, but this balloon ride is something I want both of us to share.

Our guide Rowan gets everything ready for take-off while I work on calming my boyfriend.

I take Justin's hands, squeezing them tightly. "Look at me, Justin."

Justin forces himself to look at me and I see the fear in his blue eyes. The last time I saw him get hysterical over heights was when our families took a holiday to Queensland when we were ten. I don't know exactly what happened or what made Justin suddenly feel terrified of heights, but I remember getting on a ride with him and Alyssa at Movie World. He began panicking once we reached the top of the ride. By the time we reached the bottom to get off, Justin was in tears. Since then, he never goes anywhere near high places.

"I'm going to be right here with you, Justin," I say. "Don't think about what's down below. Think about how it's going to be an amazing experience."

"You are going to be okay once we get up in the sky, mate," Rowan says. "I have had many people come on the hot air balloon tours with a fear of heights, and they pretty much forget about their fear once they are up in the air. I promise you will be safe."

Justin doesn't look very convinced.

I rest a hand on Justin's cheek. "See, Justin. Even Rowan said you are going to be fine once we get up. Just do this once for the both of us."

Justin inhales a deep breath and lets it out slowly, his breath shaky. "Okay. I will do this. For us."

I smile at him and peck him on the lips. "I promise you won't regret it."

Rowan turns on the gas and drops the sandbags on the ground so the balloon can start rising once Justin has calmed down. The sun begins to rise, and Justin decides to keep his eyes closed until we are up in the air, hanging on tightly to the edge of the basket. Once up in the air, I put my hand over his where they are still holding onto the edge of the basket and tell him to open his eyes.

He hesitates at first. But he listens, opening them to see an amazing view of the Yarra Valley landscape. It's even more beautiful with the sunrise.

"Wow," he says.

"So? How are you feeling?"

He turns to look at me. I can still see the fear in his eyes, but it's starting to subside. "Apart from my heart racing a million miles per hour, I think I'm okay."

"I told you, Justin, that you will be okay once we are in the air," Rowan says.

Justin looks over at him. "Yeah, you did."

Rowan smiles. "If it makes you feel any better, I used to be afraid of heights myself. In fact, a ride in a hot air balloon is what helped me get over the fear."

"How many years have you been flying hot air balloons?" I ask him.

"I have been doing this for eight years now," he says. "It's honestly the best job in the world, taking all kinds of people up in the air so they can enjoy the fantastic views."

I glance down at the valley, the farmlands, vineyards and lakes looking so amazing with a bird's-eye view of the whole Yarra Valley. I feel so incredibly lucky to have this chance, because, honestly, I don't think I would have ever thought of doing something like this. It almost makes me feel bad for dumping Oliver, even though he was a complete asshole for cheating on me. At the same time, he was thoughtful in putting together this trip. But even if I wasn't spending this weekend getaway with my ex, I was spending it with my best friend in the entire world. I couldn't imagine having this opportunity with anyone other than Justin.

Justin begins to relax about being in the air, just like Rowan said he would. He puts an arm around my waist.

"You know, Am, as much as your ex is a douchebag, I'm glad he allowed us to go on this trip together," Justin tells me. "Although a hot air balloon ride is probably something I wouldn't have done, this weekend has been really great."

I rest my head on his shoulder. "I agree. I don't want it to ever end."

"It doesn't have to end. We should plan another weekend away together, or maybe even go on holidays for a week or two. Maybe we should look into doing a cruise like your parents?"

I look up at him with a smile. "I like that idea."

Justin returns a smile and pulls me in for a passionate kiss.

Chapter Nine

The end of a work day is always my favourite. It's not because I don't like my job – I love it – but near the end of the day it excites me knowing that I will be seeing Justin. And after the weekend we had enjoyed together, it was back to reality.

Justin waits outside the café while I clean up inside and say goodbye to Stacey and my other co-workers. He is looking at his phone when I come out of the café, leaning his back against the wall, probably browsing his social media. He slips his phone in his pocket when he sees me. I hold up his coffee and he smiles, taking it, giving me a peck on the cheek.

"I also got you a strawberry iced doughnut to go with your coffee," I say, holding up the brown paper bag.

Justin takes the bag. "Oh, thank you. You're the best, Am."

I hold his coffee so he can take out the doughnut. He takes

a huge bite out of it before tossing the paper bag in a nearby bin. He then takes the coffee cup from me, walking down the street, eating the doughnut.

"How was your day?" I ask him.

Justin nods, enjoying every moment of the doughnut. "Good, good. I'm just happy to be able to go home and spend the evening with you." He stuffs the last part of the doughnut into his mouth and wraps his arm around my shoulders. "How was your day?"

"Other than a few rude customers, it was good."

"I was thinking that after the weekend we had that we should have a relaxing one. Maybe we could order in. What do you say?"

"I love that idea. What are you thinking?"

He takes a sip of his coffee. "I was thinking Thai."

"Thai sounds good."

"Thai it is."

We step out onto the road to cross to the tram stop. Just as we do, a car comes speeding around the corner, not slowing down for the crossing. Everything happens so fast as Justin pushes me out of the way. Justin doesn't get out of the way fast enough and is struck by the car. His body falls onto the bonnet, his head smashing the windscreen, and then rolls off as the car speeds away.

"Justin!" I scream.

Witnesses come rushing over to Justin. My body shakes as I see my boyfriend lying lifeless on the road on his back, his right leg sticking out at an odd angle. There's a gash on his forehead. Someone is on the phone, calling for an ambulance. I push my way to Justin and take his hand, squeezing it.

I beg him to wake up, but he doesn't.

* * *

My entire world completely stops all around me as I try to process what's happening.

Justin's heart stops beating in the back of the ambulance. I watch as the paramedic uses the defibrillator on him. His heart starts beating again on the second charge, and I let out the breath I was unaware of holding.

Once at the hospital, Justin is rushed to the ER. I sit in the waiting room and call Justin's parents to inform them of the accident. I also call my sister, because she's the one person I really need right now.

Elise and Darren are the first ones to get to the hospital. Elise rushes over to me and pulls me into a hug.

"Have you heard anything about what's going on?" Darren asks me as he stands beside his wife.

I shake my head, wiping my eyes. "I don't know. I think he is still in surgery."

"I will go and see if I can get any information."

Darren walks over to the reception to see if he can find out what's happening with his son.

Elise turns to me, her face wet with tears. She pats my cheek. "Are you okay, Amberlee? What happened?"

I can't tell her without breaking down into tears, replaying the moment in my head. Thankfully, Darren returns so I don't have to answer, wrapping me into a hug, rubbing a hand up and down my back to soothe me.

"What did the receptionist say?" Elise asks her husband.

"She said she will find someone who can come down to explain Justin's situation," he says.

"I'm so sorry you guys," I say. "It all happened so fast. We were crossing the road and then the next minute a car just came speeding around the corner. It didn't even slow down for the people who were already at the crossing. Justin pushed me out of the way before the car hit him."

"There's no need to apologise, Amberlee." He strokes my hair. "The person who hit him should have slowed down."

Anger rises in me at the thought of the driver. "They didn't even stop! They just kept driving, not caring if they left Justin for dead."

My heart aches. If anything happens to Justin, there is no way I can live without him. All I can do is pray that he makes it through. His heart has stopped once, and I won't be able to bear it if it stops a second time.

"Amberlee!"

I pull away from Darren and see Alyssa hurrying over to me. "I came as soon as I could," she says, pulling me into a hug.

I notice my nephew isn't with her. She should have been picking him up from childcare when I called her. "Where's Mickey?"

"I have my next door neighbour watching him." She pulls away from me and cups her hands around my face, forcing me to look at her. "Are you okay, Amberlee? You aren't hurt?"

I shake my head. "No. But Justin is badly injured. His heart stopped in the ambulance, but the paramedics brought him back. He is in surgery right now."

We sit down, waiting up to an hour, maybe more, for news about how Justin is. Finally, a doctor comes out to talk to us.

"He is stable," the doctor tells us. "We have put him in an induced coma. His right leg is completely shattered with a broken thigh and leg, along with a broken hip." Elise gasps at the doctor's words. "He will have to go through therapy to walk again. His left collarbone is also broken. The good news is that there was no internal bleeding and no brain injury. I can't tell you how long he will be in this coma for, but he is currently in a stable condition. I have been told his heart stopped in the ambulance, but I can assure you he is alright now. We just need him to recover so he can come out of the coma."

"Can we see him now?" Elise asks.

"Just two people at a time." He looks at Alyssa and I. "Are you two family?"

I shake my head. "I'm his girlfriend and this is my sister."

"Okay, well, I'm afraid at this time I can only allow family into the room."

I want to protest, but at the same time I know there's no point.

Darren turns to me. "Why don't you go home with your sister? I will give you a call and let you know when you can come see Justin."

All I could do was nod. Although I would much rather wait at the hospital than go home. But I guess going home would be better than waiting around the hospital where Justin could wake up from his coma at any time – a few days, weeks...

Or maybe never.

No. I refuse to think that at all. Justin is going to wake up from this. We are soulmates. He can't just leave me behind.

Alyssa takes me home to her place. It's probably best because I'm sure I wouldn't be able to handle being in my own house without thinking about Justin, wouldn't be able to handle going to bed without him. We drive home in complete silence.

Mickey is excited to see me, but I'm not feeling up to playing with my nephew. I just want to be alone. I force a smile and hug him. Then I wander off to the guest room and lie down on the bed, hugging a pillow as I cry myself to sleep.

Chapter Ten

I'm pretty sure the world has stopped.

Okay, maybe not the world, but *my* world. Nothing felt right without Justin. I can't find a way to get out of bed after my sleepless night.

I wonder what would have happened if Justin hadn't saved me in time. Would I be the one in a coma instead of Justin? How would Justin react to me being in the hospital? The thoughts scare me and I really don't want to keep thinking about it all.

I force myself out of bed and start the day by contacting Justin's boss to let them know what happened. I then ask my boss if it's alright for me to have the day off. There's no way I can focus on work when my boyfriend is in the hospital, not knowing if he will make it or not.

Alyssa comes to check in on me as soon as I get off the phone with my boss.

"Hey," she says with a small smile.

"Morning, Alyssa."

"Are you going to work today?"

I shake my head. "No. There is no way I can work while Justin is on my mind."

"Have his parents contacted you yet?"

I shake my head. "No, not yet."

"Maybe you can go down to the hospital today. You might be able to see him his time. And even if you still aren't allowed to, I'm sure Darren and Elise will let you see him anyway."

"I don't understand how we had this perfect getaway over the weekend for my birthday, and then this happened."

Alyssa rests her hand on my arm. "Things happened that are beyond your control. What happened to Justin could have been anyone. You both were just in the wrong place at the wrong time."

I nod, and agree to go to the hospital.

"For now, why don't you come to the kitchen and have something to eat?" Alyssa says. "You didn't have anything to eat last night and I didn't want to wake you when you fell asleep."

"I don't know if I have the appetite to eat."

"Just have something anyway, even if it's a little bit. After breakfast you can go and freshen up. You can borrow something from me, unless you want me to drop you off at your place to change."

"Thanks, Alyssa." I give my sister a small smile. "I will just wear something from you."

"And if you want, I will drive you to the hospital and we

can see Justin together."

"Alyssa, you have work today. I can't let you take the day off to be with me just because my boyfriend is in hospital."

"Amberlee, it's okay. I'm your big sister. My job is to make sure you're okay. It will be no problem at all."

I wrap my sister into a hug. "Thank you, Alyssa."

* * *

An hour later, Alyssa drops me at the hospital. She was still persisting to come in with me, but I told her I wanted to go in on my own. She told me to message her later when I want to leave, but, truthfully, I was thinking of catching the tram home so I could be alone with my thoughts.

Elise meets me out front and leads me to Justin's room. She looks like a total mess, her greying brown hair tied in a messy bun and her eyes all red and puffy. She looks like she hasn't had a wink of sleep, and I can't blame her.

"How is he?" I ask as we stand in front of a lift.

Elise presses the button. "He hasn't changed."

I wrap Elise into a hug, letting go as soon as the lift doors open. She presses the level number and then leads me to the ICU.

Darren is sitting beside Justin when I walk in. He looks up when the two of us enter the room. He stands and tells me to sit beside Justin, then he leaves the room with his wife so we can be alone.

I sit down in the chair beside Justin's bed. I bite down on my lip to stop myself from crying at the sight of my boyfriend. Justin's right leg is elevated and his left arm is in a sling. He has tubes to help him breathe and all sorts of wires hooked up to monitor his condition.

A small cry escapes my lips when I see him. "Oh, Justin."

I reach out and take Justin's hand. I've heard you can talk to coma patients and they can hear everything you tell them, but I don't know what to say. I feel bad that he's here instead of me. I should be the one lying in the bed, fighting for my life. But instead, Justin saved me. I wonder for a second what would've happened if we had only just waited for a few minutes before crossing the street.

"Thank you, Justin, for saving me," I tell him. "I keep replaying everything back in my head, and I wish I could change it so you aren't here right now."

It's no use trying to hold the tears back because they begin to flow on their own. "Please, wake up, Justin. I don't want to lose you. I can't live without you."

I stare at every inch of him, watching for some kind of movement like maybe he will wake up when he hears my voice, or he will answer me. But he shows no sign of waking up. I tell myself not to think the worst. Justin is going to wake up. He needs to.

For me.

***

Later that week, I get a call from Elise just after midday while I'm on my lunch break. She tells me to come down to the hospital when I can. She wouldn't tell me if Justin was okay. She just wanted me to get to the hospital as soon as I can.

I ask my boss if I can have an extended lunch break. He allows me to and I head off. My head races with all kind of thoughts on the tram to the hospital. Is Justin okay? He has been in a coma for four days. Did he wake up? *Oh please, God, please tell me he woke up.*

I walk as fast as I can down the corridor to the ICU and enter the room. There, lying in his bed with the ventilator on, I see Justin's eyes are opened. His parents are standing beside his bed, smiling.

"Justin!" I cry out.

He turns his head towards me. I hurry into the room and wrap my arms around him, careful not to hurt him.

Justin can't talk or smile with the ventilator. But he reaches for me with his good hand and squeezes mine. I kiss his knuckles. Happy tears fill my eyes. Justin lets go of my hand and rests his on my cheek, wiping away the tears falling down my face.

I smile at him, glad to have him back.

Chapter Eleven

Four months later

Justin was in the hospital for a week. He wasn't able to get around on crutches, so he had to remain in a wheelchair for six weeks until his leg had healed.

Elise came around during the week to help take care of him while I had work or classes. Darren also helped out with Justin, and I was thankful for their help. There was no way I could take care of Justin on my own. Alyssa came over on weekends to help me out with anything, and even my parents came over to help once they returned from their holiday. Justin's boss allowed him to work from home until he was able to go back to the office.

Whenever I could, I went with Justin to doctor and physio appointments. It had taken him twelve weeks to recover from his injuries. Some days, Justin got frustrated with himself as he learned to walk again. I assured him that everything will be fine.

We spend every moment we can together, even if we can only cuddle on the bed where Justin often feels most comfortable. Every night we settle on the bed with my laptop and watch Netflix. Spending every moment with him made me appreciate what he did to save me from being hit by the car.

It also made me appreciate him still being here. I couldn't imagine my life without Justin. He was my best friend, my soulmate.

One winter afternoon, Justin suggests we take a walk around the Royal Botanical Gardens.

It's the first time we've gone out somewhere other than to attend doctor appointments. Justin can't walk long distances without feeling pain from his hip. He limps whenever he walks. The doctor said he won't fully recover for a year. In the meantime, Justin is taking everything slow.

"Let me know when you need to take a rest," I tell him as we walk along the path in the gardens.

He gives me a small smile. "I'm fine, Am. You don't need to keep worrying about me." He puts an arm around my waist. "But don't worry, I will let you know when I need to rest. Maybe when we get to the lake we can take a rest."

I glance around at the gardens, feeling peaceful with Justin, listening to birds that were hiding in the trees.

"I haven't been here in ages," I say. "I'm glad you suggested that we come out here."

"I'm glad too. I just felt that today we needed to do something other than running around to physio appointments all the time. I also miss being able to do the things I could do before the accident. Maybe I can't quite walk long distance yet, but I just thought being out here will be great. I have been thinking that once I fully cover from my injuries that we should go on holidays somewhere."

I nod in agreement. "A getaway will be great. Any places you are thinking we should go to?"

He shakes his head. "I don't know yet. I'm thinking maybe we could travel somewhere in Australia."

"Where in Australia do you think we should go?"

Justin shrugs. "Queensland maybe? Or South Australia? I don't know yet. We should look at places where we can go. Somewhere we haven't been to before. Maybe we could go during the Christmas break."

We reach the lake and head over to the water's edge. We sit down on the grass, admiring some black swans on the water. It's such a beautiful day with the sun shining brightly. It may be winter, but it's warm out.

"Amberlee, we have been dating for five months now," Justin says. "When I was hit by that car in March, I realise just how lucky I was to make it through. It made me wonder about our future together. Not just as friends, but more than that. Kissing you that Valentine's night was the best decision I have ever made. If I hadn't taken you out that night, maybe I would never have made the decision to make a move on you."

I smile, thinking about the night. It was a move I'm definitely glad we made.

Justin pulls something out of the pocket of his jeans. He turns to me. "You are the best friend I could ever ask for and I can't imagine my life without you."

My heart stops when I see the small black box in his hand.

"That's why I am asking you, Amberlee Jessa Jones, if you will marry me?"

Justin opens the box, revealing a silver ring with an oval diamond in the centre and smaller diamonds around the band. I gasp.

I nod as tears spring to my eyes. I never thought this would happen. "Yes! I will marry you, Justin."

Justin slips the ring onto my finger. I hold my hand in front of me, the diamond glittering when the sun shines on it. It's perfect.

I look up at Justin and kiss him passionately.

Who knew that spending one whole night together could change our lives forever.

Acknowledgements

One Whole Night with You

The people I would like to thank who had helped me put this story together is the writing community on Twitter, especially Leonie Rhule. When I was struggling to write for the past three months due to being unwell and being under a lot of stress, Leonie and other people in the writing community helped me to keep my head up when I was in self-doubt with my work, and it helped me to write the story I wanted to tell. Without Leonie's help, I don't think I would have had the encouragement I needed to get the words down.

And of course, thank you to Avery McDougall for helping with the edits, sharing your thoughts on how to make this book what it is.

Every Moment with You

I never really expected to write this short novelette series about two friends falling for each other, but it's something I'm quite proud I have written, especially while going through a writing slump. The one person who has been there by my side, even when we are half way across the world from each other, is Leonie Rhule. I owe a huge thank you to her. She has been a great friend to me on bookstagam, and when I have been struggling with my writing, she would always give me good advice that would help me get back into writing. I wasn't even sure if I should go ahead and publish this sequel that I wrote for fun, and Leonie encouraged me to get it out there.

Thank you also to my readers for picking up this book and giving it a chance. I hope you enjoyed Justin's and Amberlee's journey. And thank you to my editor Emily for working on this story with me. I really appreciate it.

About the Author

Jessica Madden was born and raised in Sydney, Australia. She began writing stories since the age of eight. When she was nine, she realised that she wanted to be a writer more than anything in the world. At twenty-three years old, Jessica published her first book *Right Here Waiting for You*. Writing about characters falling in love has always been her favourite thing to write about.

When she is not writing, Jessica is often daydreaming up new storylines, and can be found lost in reading a good book.

You can follow her on Twitter and Instagram
@JessicaCMadden

Also by Jessica Madden

Right Here Waiting for You
The Jet Lag Diaries
Silent Love
Chasing the Storm
If You Had Stayed
Hating Jamie Jackson

I Wasn't Supposed to Fall for You

I Wasn't Supposed to Fall for You
It's All Because Of You

With You

One Whole Night with You
Every Moment with You